A REPUTATION THAT STRETCHED FOR MILES...

When Frank Gardner entered the bar he wasn't looking for Beatrice, but there she was, sitting with a man. Was she trying to make him jealous? He smiled, waved, and walked over to them.

"Introduce me to your friend, Bea," Gardner said.

"Frank," she said, "this is an old friend of my father's . . ."

"Nice to meet you," Gardner said, extending his hand.

". . . Clint Adams," she finished.

Gardner's hand faltered, but he regrouped and completed the handshake. . . .

DON'T MISS THESE
ALL-ACTION WESTERN SERIES
FROM THE BERKLEY PUBLISHING GROUP

THE GUNSMITH by J. R. Roberts
Clint Adams was a legend among lawmen, outlaws, and ladies.
They called him . . . the Gunsmith.

LONGARM by Tabor Evans
The popular long-running series about U.S. Deputy Marshal
Long—his life, his loves, his fight for justice.

SLOCUM by Jake Logan
Today's longest-running action Western. John Slocum rides a
deadly trail of hot blood and cold steel.

BUSHWHACKERS by B. J. Lanagan
An action-packed series by the creators of Longarm! The rousing
adventures of the most brutal gang of cutthroats ever assembled—
Quantrill's Raiders.

THE GUNSMITH

205

THE GAMBLER'S GIRL

J. R. ROBERTS

JOVE BOOKS, NEW YORK

THE GAMBLER'S GIRL

A Jove Book / published by arrangement with
the author

PRINTING HISTORY
Jove edition / February 1999

The Penguin Putnam Inc. World Wide Web site address is
http://www.penguinputnam.com

ISBN: 0-515-12451-6

A JOVE BOOK®
Jove Books are published by The Berkley Publishing Group,
a member of Penguin Putnam Inc.,
375 Hudson Street, New York, New York 10014.
JOVE and the "J" design
are trademarks belonging to Jove Publications, Inc.

PRINTED IN THE UNITED STATES OF AMERICA

10 9 8 7 6 5 4 3 2 1

ONE

It had been some time since Clint had last seen his friend Howard Haskell. The telegram that reached him in Labyrinth, Texas, sounded frantic, so Clint left the very next day for Haskell's West Texas ranch.

Howard Haskell was one of the finest horse breeders in Texas, maybe even the West, and as such he had amassed an impressive fortune. Clint knew him before he became so wealthy and was impressed when he rode up to Haskell's ranch house. The last time he'd been there the house had been a simple two-room wooden affair hand built by Haskell himself. Of course, the last time he was there Haskell's wife, Beverly, had still been alive.

Now the house was still made of wood, but it was the finest cured wood money could buy, and it stood two stories high and had ten or twelve rooms, at least.

"Mr. Adams?"

Clint had just reined Duke in, in front of the house, when he heard his name. He dismounted and turned to face a man in his thirties who was approaching him.

"You are Clint Adams, aren't you?"

"That's right."

"I figured there couldn't be two black geldings that

1

size," the man said. He put out his hand. "I'm Keith Abel, Mr. Haskell's foreman."

"Mr. Abel," Clint said, shaking the man's hand.

"Just call me Keith," the man said. "Everyone else does."

"All right, Keith, I'm Clint."

"And this is Duke, eh?"

"That's him."

"I've heard about him, but I never expected him to be this impressive."

"Do you have someone who can take care of him for me?" Clint asked. "He's a handful."

"We've got a few men who are good handlers," Abel said, "but if you don't mind I'll take you in to see Mr. Haskell, and then I'll take care of your horse myself."

"Hell, I don't mind," Clint said, "just so long as you know what you're letting yourself in for."

"I'll take my chances," Abel said. "Shall we go in? Mr. Haskell is pretty anxious."

"Lead the way," Clint said and followed Abel into the house. "His telegram sure sounded anxious. What's it all about?"

Over his shoulder Abel said, "If you don't mind I'll let him tell you about it. After all, it is his private business."

"But you know about it."

"Well, I'm the foreman," Abel said. "A good foreman knows everything that goes on around a ranch."

Clint couldn't very well argue with that.

Keith Abel led Clint through the house, all of the rooms of which were expensively furnished. Haskell had done even better for himself than Clint had realized, given the size of the house and the spread.

"This is Mr. Haskell's office," Abel said and led Clint into the room. "Clint Adams is here, sir."

"Clint!" Haskell leaped up from behind his desk and

charged forward with his hand out. "It's been years, boy, goddamned years!"

His friend's appearance shocked Clint. It had been ten or eleven years since he'd seen him, but the man seemed to have aged twenty. His once sandy hair had turned white. His once powerfully built body had grown lean, almost frail-looking.

"What is it, ten, eleven years?" Haskell asked.

"That's what I was just thinking."

"Have a seat," Haskell said. "You've met Keith?"

"We introduced ourselves."

"Keith, why don't you have a seat, too?" Haskell asked his foreman.

"I promised Clint I'd take care of his horse personally, Boss," Abel said. "Besides, I know this is gonna be kind of personal. I'll see you both later."

With that Abel left the room.

"He's a good man," Haskell said. Clint had to take his word for it.

"I know what you're thinking," the man said.

"Do you?"

"Yeah," Haskell said. "I look like shit."

"Well . . ."

"Don't deny it," Haskell said, going back around his desk and sitting down. "I know I look like shit. I've gone downhill since Bev died."

"I'm sorry about that, Howard," Clint said, recalling that she had died about seven years before. He had sent his condolences in a telegram. He'd meant to visit soon after, but time had gotten away from him.

"And now this," Haskell said. "How am I going to withstand this?"

"Withstand what, Howard?" Clint asked. "You don't have to read my mind to know that I'm wondering why I'm here."

"It's Beatrice."

"Your daughter?"

Haskell nodded.

"Good God, she must be . . . twenty now?"

"Twenty-one."

"And does she look like Bev?"

"Spittin' image."

"That means she's beautiful."

"She is," Haskell said, "but that's only part of the problem."

"What's the other part?"

"She's gone, Clint," Haskell said. "She's gone."

TWO

"What do you mean gone, Howard?" Clint asked. "Has she been kidnapped?"

"Not exactly."

"What's that mean, 'not exactly'?" he asked. "Did she go off on her own?"

"Well . . . no, not exactly."

"Howard," Clint said, "help me out here. All you're doing is confusing me."

"She met a man a few months ago," Haskell said, "when he came to town."

The largest and nearest town to Haskell's ranch was El Paso.

"El Paso?"

"Yes."

"Who was the man?"

"His name is Frank Gardner," Haskell said. "He is a gambler, handsome, older than she."

"How much older?"

"Younger than me, but old enough to be her father," Haskell said.

Clint realized that could have described him—the last line, anyway.

"And what happened, Howard?"

"He cast some sort of spell over her."

"Howard—"

"Well, you know what I mean," the man said. "I don't mean it was magic, but it was . . . something. All she could think about was him. She wanted to be with him all the time. Finally, she left the ranch and moved in with him at the El Paso Hotel."

"And that's where she is now?" Clint asked. "Then what do you mean she's gone?"

"No," Haskell said, "she's not there anymore. They left there."

"And went where?"

"That's just it," Haskell said, spreading his hands helplessly. "I don't know where they went!"

"She didn't tell you?"

"No," Haskell said, shaking his head mournfully.

"Did she even tell you she was leaving?"

"Yes," he said. "She came to the ranch and said she and Frank had to leave. When I asked where, she said she couldn't tell me. When I asked why, she said Frank said she couldn't tell me."

"And she accepted that?"

"Yes."

Clint rubbed his jaw. Maybe the man *had* cast some sort of spell over her.

"So they left?"

Haskell nodded.

"When was this?"

"Two months ago," Haskell said. "I became frantic. I hired detectives to find them, but no one could."

"I guess you hired the wrong detectives," Clint said. "Talbot Roper is the best in the business. I could give you his address in Denver—"

"No," he said, "I'm through with detectives. I want you to find her."

"Me? But I'm not a detective."

"You're better than a detective," Haskell said. "You know men like Frank Gardner."

Clint frowned. He knew men like that, yes, but the name Gardner did not ring a bell with him at all.

"Well, I could wire some people and see if they know him," Clint said. "Bat Masterson, Luke Short . . . one of them might have heard of him."

"See, already there's something you can do that a detective couldn't."

"Howard, all I said was I'd send some wires—"

"You've got to help me, Clint," Haskell said. "I'm going crazy. I need to know where she is, that she's all right. I'm beggin' you!"

"You don't have to beg me, Howard," Clint said. He was annoyed that Haskell was putting him in this position, but he couldn't very well turn his friend down.

"All right," Clint said finally, "I'll see what I can do. I'll check around El Paso and send some telegrams from there."

"You could stay here while you wait for the replies—" Haskell started.

"No," Clint said, "somebody in El Paso might know where they went. I'll want to ask around there while I wait for the replies. You said he was there three months?"

"Around that."

"Then he must have made friends with somebody," Clint said. "That's where I'll have to start."

Clint stood up. Haskell did, too, and rushed around his desk to grab Clint's hand and pump it furiously.

"I really appreciate this, Clint," he said. "I know you can find her."

"I'll do the best I can, Howard, but it might mean some traveling—"

"I'll cover all your expenses."

"That's not what I meant—"

"I don't care," Haskell said. "You just tell me how much you need and you'll have it."

"I don't need anything yet," Clint said, retrieving his hand. "All I'm going to do is take a room at the El Paso Hotel and send some wires."

"I'll take care of the hotel," Haskell said. "It's the least I can do. I'll send Keith in with you to handle it."

"Howard—"

"He has to go into El Paso anyway," Haskell said quickly. "Let him ride with you."

"Fine," Clint said, "he can ride with me."

Haskell walked Clint to the front door and went outside with him. He snagged a hand who was passing by and told him to find Keith Abel.

"Have a seat," Haskell said, indicating some wicker chairs on the porch. "I'll be back with Keith and your horse."

Clint nodded and sat down in one of the comfortable chairs. He tried to remember what Beatrice had looked like the last time he saw her. All he could conjure up were some knobby knees, freckles, and pigtails. How was that going to help him find her? He was going to have to see if Haskell had some recent photographs. More and more people were getting their photographs taken these days. He still had never done it, himself, and hadn't allowed any to be taken. He knew they'd eventually find their way into some newspaper.

He could see how a girl—or a young woman, since she was twenty-one—could be taken in by an older, wiser man, a gambler who seemed romantic, but it wasn't right to take a young woman like that away from her father and not let him know where she was. Clint could only imagine how he'd feel if he had a daughter and it happened to him.

Suddenly, he was dead set on finding Beatrice Haskell.

THREE

The first time Clint had been to El Paso, Texas, the marshal had been Dallas Stoudenmire. He'd helped Stoudenmire out of a tight spot, but since then the lawman had gotten himself killed. Clint read about it, not long after the whole business in Tombstone with the Earps and the Clantons. Seemed a lot was happening at that time.

He'd been back once since then and had found some trouble on the Mexican side of the town. El Paso still looked sleepy to him, and he was determined to remain on the American side this trip. According to Haskell, that was where Gardner and his daughter had stayed.

The ride to El Paso from the ranch was uneventful and would have been peaceful if Keith Abel hadn't been along. The foreman was a talkative cuss, and it wasn't even that he was nosy and asked a lot of questions or that he talked about himself a lot—he simply liked to talk.

"Did you know Frank Gardner?" Clint asked, along the way. At that point he figured if the man wanted to talk he might answer a few questions.

"I met him," Abel said. "Didn't get to know him real well."

"What did you think of him?"

"Honestly?"

9

"That's why I asked."

"I didn't like him."

"Why not?"

"I didn't think he was right for Bea—I mean, Beatrice."

"Why not?"

"Well, for one thing he was too old for her," Abel said.

"How old was he?"

"About your age—oh, no offense."

"None taken."

"I just don't think a girl Bea's age—I mean, Beatrice—should have taken up with a man so—well, I mean, uh, his age."

Clint had the feeling there was more to it than that. It wouldn't be the first time a foreman had fallen for the boss's daughter.

"And then there was what he did for a living."

"Gambling?"

"Poker, to be exact."

"You don't like poker players?"

Abel looked away for a moment. Clint had the feeling he was looking at something only he could see. It turned out to be something from his past.

"My father played poker," he finally said. "He left me and my mom alone a lot."

"But he came home, didn't he?"

"Oh, yeah," Abel said, "he came home—except for the last time, when he was playing poker and somebody accused him of cheating."

"What happened?"

"They killed him."

"Was he cheating?"

"I never knew," Abel said. "All I know is that everybody who was in the game took him outside and beat him to death."

"Where did that happen?"

"Caldwell, Kansas."

Clint frowned. This sounded familiar.

"How long ago?"

"Twenty years or more."

"Abel," Clint said to himself, then raised his eyebrows. "Was your father . . . Jack Abel?"

Now it was the other man's turn to be surprised.

"You knew my father?"

"Can't say I *knew* him, actually," Clint said. "Knew of him, heard of him, met him once."

"When? Where?"

Suddenly, Keith Abel seemed very anxious for this information.

Clint frowned. Try as he might, he couldn't remember where or under what circumstances he had met the man.

"I can't recall right now, Keith. I'm really sorry about this."

"Try," Abel said, "please."

"It'll come to me while I'm here. I know it will," Clint said. "When it does I'll let you know."

"I'd appreciate it," Abel said. "It's real important to me."

"Why?" Clint asked. "I mean, if you don't mind me saying so, you don't sound like you really liked your dad all that much."

"I spent years hating him, but . . . like I said before, I never knew if he was actually cheating or not. I'd like to know for sure."

"I wasn't there, Keith," Clint said. "That's the one thing I can tell you. It wasn't Caldwell, Kansas, where I met him."

"Maybe not," Keith Abel said anxiously, "but maybe you'll remember something that will tell you whether or not he was a cheater."

"Well . . . I'll try," Clint said, "that's all I can promise."

"That's all I can ask."

It took another half hour of riding after that to reach El Paso, and Keith Abel was quiet the entire way.

FOUR

When they reached town they split up so that Abel could go and run his errands.

"I'll stop at the El Paso first thing and tell them that Mr. Haskell will be paying your bill," he promised. "The boss made me promise to do that before I did anything else."

"Thanks," Clint said. He'd decided not to argue the point.

"Maybe we could have a drink later?" Abel asked. "Before I head back?"

"Sure," Clint said, even though he figured Abel might be expecting him to remember by then where he had met his father.

Clint rode to the livery and left Duke in the hands of the liveryman, then walked to the El Paso Hotel and got himself a room. True to his word, Abel had already been there, and since a big, wealthy rancher like Howard Haskell was paying the bill, the clerk treated Clint very well.

"Can I have someone carry your saddlebags to your room, sir?" he asked.

"No, that's fine," Clint said. "I carried them this far myself, I can carry them the rest of the way."

"Very well, sir," the fussy little man said. "If I can do

anything at all for you, please let me know.''

"I will," Clint said. "I promise."

Clint took his saddlebags and rifle up to the room, then came back down and went in search of a meal. Over a steak at a small café he tried to decide what his next move should be. First, of course, he would send out the telegrams to his friends, asking if any of them knew Frank Gardner. Bat, Wyatt, even Rick Hartman in Labyrinth, someone was bound to have heard of the man. Hell, they might even know where he was. That would certainly make the whole process of locating Beatrice Haskell a lot easier.

If, however, things were not that easy he'd have to check in the saloons, find out where Gardner was playing poker while he was here, then find the people he was playing with and see if any of them knew anything.

There had to be a clue to Frank Gardner's whereabouts in El Paso somewhere. If there wasn't, this was going to be *real* difficult.

FIVE

After his meal Clint went directly to the telegraph office and sent out half a dozen wires. Along with Bat, Wyatt, Luke Short, and Rick Hartman, he included Buckskin Frank Leslie and Ben Thompson. He and Thompson weren't exactly friends, but Ben was a gambler and knew almost every other gambler of note in the country. Of all of these people, he expected to get something from either Ben or Rick Hartman.

Once the telegrams were sent and the clerk knew where to deliver the replies, he started visiting El Paso's saloons and gambling emporiums. After two or three he found Keith Abel at the bar of the Lucky Lady.

"Clint! Come have that drink," Abel called out as he entered.

Clint cringed because he wasn't exactly letting everyone in town know who he was. He got to Abel before the man could call out anything else.

"Don't call out my name like that," he said. "You could get me killed."

"Oops," Abel said, hunching his shoulders, "sorry. I didn't think."

"What'll ya have?" the bartender asked.

15

"A beer," Clint said, "and bring my friend another one."

"Comin' up."

"Did you remember anything?" Abel asked.

"About?" Clint said.

"My father," Abel said. "Did you remember where you met him?"

Clint closed his eyes. He'd already forgotten the conversation they'd had earlier.

"No, it hasn't come to me yet, Keith. I'm sorry."

"Well, keep thinking about it."

"I will."

"Did you get those telegrams sent?"

"I did," Clint said. "When the replies come they'll be delivered to me at the hotel. Did you get all your errands done?"

"Yep," Abel said. "I just wanted to have a beer with you before I went back."

On cue the bartender returned and set down two beers on the bar.

"Well," Abel said, picking up the fresh one, "here's to your success."

"Thanks, Keith."

"Yup," he said, "I hope you remember where you met my father real soon." He drank down half the beer and put the mug on the bar. "See you before you leave, Clint."

"Bye, Keith."

Abel left the bar and Clint called the bartender over.

"Somethin' wrong?"

"Do you run a poker game here?"

"We don't run one," the barman said, "but one or two usually break out each night."

"You remember a gambler named Frank Gardner who was in town for a few months?"

"The one who left town with Howard Haskell's daughter? Sure do."

"Does everyone in town know about this?" Clint asked.

"Word gets around."

"Did Gardner play poker here?"

The heavyset bartender stroked his jowls for a few moments and then shook his head.

"Can't say I ever remember him playing here."

"Well, he must have played someplace."

"Where have ya checked?"

Clint told him the names of three other saloons in town.

"You ain't checked the Golden Nickel yet?"

"Not yet."

"Most of the poker in town goes on there."

"Is that a fact? Well, I'll have to check that one next. Thanks for the information."

"Sure."

"I wonder why none of the bartenders at the other places would tell me that?"

"They don't like to send customers to the competition," the bartender said.

"But I'm not looking for a place to gamble," Clint said. "I'm just looking for some information."

"Maybe they didn't understand that."

Clint finished the beer and put the empty mug on the bar.

"Well, I'm glad you do . . ."

"Max."

"Thanks again, Max."

"Sure thing," Max said. "By the way, when ya get to the Nickel say hello to the bartender, Milo."

"Milo? Sure. Who's that?"

"He's my brother."

"Does he own that place?"

"Sure does."

"And you own this one?"

"Yup."

Clint nodded. "I see," he said, and he finally did.

SIX

When Clint walked into the Golden Nickel he had to double-check to make sure he was not still in the Lucky Lady Saloon. The bartender looked exactly like Max. The resemblance was uncanny, even though they did not seem to be twins.

"Milo?" he asked as he approached the bar.

"That's right. What can I do for ya?"

"Your brother Max wanted me to say hello to you."

Milo put down the glass he was cleaning and put his hand out.

"Max sent ya, huh? Glad ta know ya . . . ?"

"Clint."

They shook hands.

"What can I do for ya? Beer?"

"Sure, why not?"

Milo drew him a beer and set it down in front of him.

"I was looking for some information about a gambler named Gardner, Frank Gardner."

"The fella that ran off with Howard Haskell's daughter?" Milo said.

"That's the one."

"You're in luck."

"Why's that?"

19

"This is where he done his gambling while he was in town."

"In a game you ran?"

"Nope," Milo said, "he usually got his own game goin' each night."

"Can you tell me who he played with?"

"Well," Milo said, rubbing his jowls as his brother had done, "there was players in and out of the game, but I think I can point out two or three regulars for ya."

"Are they here now?"

"Naw," Milo said, "nobody's here now. It's still too early. These fellers are the drinkers, not the gamblers. Those fellers will be in later."

"Well," Clint said, "maybe I'll be back around later and you can point them out when they come in?"

"Sure," Milo said, "I can do that."

"I appreciate it."

"Hey," Milo said, "anybody my brother Max sends over here is okay with me."

He still charged Clint for the beer, though. He paid for it and went back to his hotel to see if any replies to his telegrams had come in yet.

When Clint reached the hotel the desk clerk handed him two telegrams. One was from Bat, and the other from Wyatt. Neither of them had ever heard of a gambler named Frank Gardner. Both wished him luck finding the man.

Clint still felt his best chances were with Ben Thompson and Rick Hartman, so he wasn't too concerned about Bat and Wyatt's inability to help.

He went back up to his room for want of something better to do. His window overlooked the main street, and he stared down at the people going on about their business. He wondered how many of them had come into contact with Frank Gardner while he was here. Gardner sounded like a charmer. Clint couldn't help but wonder if he'd gotten involved with any other women while he was in town.

Maybe that should be his next step, question some of the women in town—maybe the girls who worked at the Golden Nickel. Just because he ended up leaving town with Beatrice Haskell didn't mean he wasn't seeing somebody else at the same time.

He decided to leave his room before he got too comfortable. There were still a couple of saloons he hadn't been to, and it wouldn't hurt anything to stop into them before he went back to the Golden Nickel.

Although Haskell had said his daughter never did it, Clint wondered if Gardner had ever gone to the Mexican side.

SEVEN

Clint returned to the Golden Nickel and got a big welcoming smile from Milo.

"You came back."

"I said I would. Are they here?"

"Two of them are," Milo said, "but they're in a game right now. Wouldn't take kindly to being interrupted right now."

"Why don't you point them out now," Clint suggested, "and I'll interrupt them later."

"That table there with four players? Man with the mustache and all the money in front of him is Denny Lehane. Fella right across from him is Harlan Coban."

"They played regularly with Gardner?"

"Four, maybe five nights a week."

"And who won?"

"Gardner."

"How often?"

Milo shrugged and said, "Four, maybe five nights a week."

"And they kept coming back for more?"

"They kept thinkin' they was gonna take him," Milo said. "You know, one more night, one more night."

"Didn't they ever get mad that he was beating them so steadily?"

"No."

"Why not?"

"Well, you'd have to ask them," Milo said, "but I think they knew he wasn't cheatin'."

"Okay," Clint said, "well, I'll talk to them later, I guess. Now maybe you can help me with something else, Milo?"

"Another drink?"

"No, not that."

"I just meant, you want another beer?"

"Oh, sure, thanks."

"Don't thank me," Milo said. "You're payin' for it."

Clint figured the fresh beer was the price of information.

"Whataya wanna know?"

"I want to know about Gardner and women."

Milo scratched his nose.

"Thought you knew, he went off with old man Haskell's daughter."

"I know that," Clint said, "but who else was he seeing while he was here? What I hear about him, he doesn't strike me as a one-woman man."

The saloon was in full swing, all the tables taken, as well as most of the spaces at the bar, and girls in bright, low-cut dresses kept crossing the room.

"See that gal in the blue dress?"

"The one with the dark hair and white skin?"

"That's her."

"He was seeing her?"

"Behind the Haskell gal's back."

"And she never found out?"

"Don't know."

Clint looked at the woman, who was at least ten years older than Beatrice Haskell.

"What's her name?"

"Darla."

"Work here long?"

"Six months or so."

"Was she in love with him?"

"Have to ask her."

"Was she all broken up when he left with Beatrice Haskell?"

"Don't know," Milo said. "I don't read women real well, but she did get real quiet for a while."

"Maybe she's over it by now."

"Maybe."

"Any other women, Milo?"

Milo didn't answer.

"Do I have to buy another beer?"

"Naw," Milo said, "I'm thinkin'. I think there was one other woman in town, but I don't know who it was."

"Did he make any male friends while he was here? I mean, besides those two poker players."

"Oh, they wasn't friends," Milo said. "Those two just looked at their poker losses like they was payin' him for some kind of private lessons."

"Well, then, did he make friends with anyone else?"

Milo scratched his nose again.

"A man's got to have somebody he talks to, Milo."

"You could try Doc."

"Is he the town doctor, or is that his name?"

"He's the doctor. Name's Owen. Gardner had a scuffle in here one night, gunned two men who accused him of cheatin'. One of them put a bullet in him. Doc dug it out. After that I think they were friends."

"Can you tell me how to get to his office?"

"Sure." Milo rattled off the directions.

Clint finished off his beer and put the empty mug down on the bar.

"Well, thanks for the information, Milo," he said. "Looks like I still have a lot of people to talk to in town."

"Well," Milo said, "just so's you didn't hear anything from me."

"You?" Clint asked. "Why, you're as quiet as a church mouse, Milo."

EIGHT

Clint decided to talk to the doctor first. He followed Milo's directions and found the office with the shingle hanging outside that said: DOCTOR JAMES OWEN.

It was late, so he knocked on the door instead of just walking in. The door was opened by a tall, white-haired man in his late fifties with dark, intense eyes.

"I was just cleaning up, getting ready to go home," the doctor said, "so unless it's an emergency or something—"

"Doctor, I wanted to talk to you about Frank Gardner," Clint said, cutting him off.

"Who?"

"You know, the gambler who ran off with Howard Haskell's daughter?"

Owen made a face and said, "Come in."

Clint entered and the doctor closed the door behind them. The office was cluttered, and Clint had the feeling it was always like that. The doctor's "cleaning up" must have had to do with something else.

"What's your name?"

"Clint Adams."

"And what's your interest in Frank Gardner?"

"Beatrice's father asked me to find her."

"You know, this town has entirely the wrong idea," Owen said.

"Maybe you can give me the right idea, Doctor."

"Nobody ran off with anyone," he said. "Frank—Mr. Gardner was leaving town, and Beatrice decided she wanted to go with him. They were in love."

"Were they?"

"Yes, they were."

"Then what was Frank Gardner doing with a saloon girl called Darla behind Beatrice's back?"

"That's just a rumor you heard from someone."

"I'm going to talk to the woman herself and see what she has to say."

"It would still just be her word."

"Doctor, am I correct in assuming that you and Frank Gardner were friends?"

"We became friends, yes."

"After you took a bullet out of him?"

"It wasn't a serious wound," Owen said. "He took a bullet in his side."

"But a friendship formed after that."

"Yes," Owen said. "He was an intelligent man and we were able to have intellectual conversations. Lord knows I couldn't find that anywhere else in El Paso."

"So if you and he were friends," Clint said, "he probably told you where he was going."

Owen hesitated, then said, "If you and I were friends, Mr. Adams, would you want me answering questions about your whereabouts?"

"Not if I asked you not to," Clint said. "Is that what happened, Doctor? He asked you not to answer questions? Is that because he doesn't want Howard Haskell to find them?"

"If Howard Haskell doesn't know where they are," Doctor Owen said, "it's because his daughter didn't tell him."

"Because Gardner wouldn't let her."

"Whatever the reason," Owen said. "Look, I've finished

talking to you, Mr. Adams. I really am getting ready to close up.''

''All right, Doctor,'' Clint said. ''Thanks for your time, anyway.''

Owen herded Clint to the door and out, closing it firmly behind him. Clint figured there was still something to be discovered from Dr. Owen, he just had to figure out how.

After finishing with the doctor he went back to his hotel to see if there were any more telegrams. There were two, one from Ben Thompson and one from Rick Hartman. Both were encouraging, in that they said basically the same thing. Both of them had heard of Frank Gardner and would put out some feelers to see if they could find out where he was. Clint was just going to have to stay put until he heard from them again.

In the case of Ben Thompson there was a little extra. His telegram said that he actually knew Frank Gardner, and he advised Clint to be careful when he found the man. Gardner, it said, was more than just a gambler.

Clint had been getting that idea already. He was apparently charming enough to attract a young woman and to make friends with an intelligent man like Dr. Owen. Also, he managed to win money from the same two men four to five nights a week, without getting them angry with him!

He stood in the lobby of the hotel and tucked the two telegrams into his shirt pocket. It was much too early to go to bed, and there was nothing to do in his room except sleep. He decided that instead of waiting for the two men to finish playing poker so he could talk to them, he'd go over to the Golden Nickel and see if that fifth seat at their table was still available.

NINE

When Clint got back to the saloon the poker game was still going on, and the fifth chair was still empty. He walked to the bar and motioned Milo over.

"Is that a private game or can anyone sit in?" he asked.

"Well, not just anyone, but if you want, I can make the introductions. They might let you sit in on my say-so."

"And why would you do that for me, Milo?" Clint asked, wondering what he had done so far to win Milo over this way.

"Because," Milo said with a smile, "then I can say that the Gunsmith played poker in my saloon."

"Well," Clint replied, "that's fair enough. Let's go over there and have you make the introductions."

Milo came around the bar and led Clint over to the poker table. He told Clint the names of the four men, but Clint only retained the two he was interested in, Coban and Lehane. Milo simply introduced him as "Clint" and said he was interested in a poker game.

"You ain't a beginner, are ya?" Lehane asked. "I hate beginners, always askin' what beats what."

"No," Clint said, "I'm not a beginner."

"All we're playin' is five-card stud," Coban said. "You got a problem with that?"

31

"No."

"Minimum bet's a dollar."

"No problem with that, either."

"Well, then, pull up a chair and it's your deal."

Clint sat down, accepted the cards, and dealt out a hand of five-card stud.

After an hour Clint was able to see why Frank Gardner had been beating these men night in and night out. They just weren't very good card players. Apparently, though, they had money, because their losses didn't seem to concern them at all. By the end of the night the other two men had tapped out, so Clint, Coban, and Lehane simply kept playing three-handed until Milo was ready to close.

Milo had been helpful in another way, as well. He started sending Darla over to the table to serve drinks. Clint didn't usually drink when he played cards, but he ordered a beer and then a second beer just so he could talk to her when she brought them and in between.

By the end of the night she was smiling at him and calling him Clint, and the two men were also calling him by name. They seemed very happy to be losing money to him. Maybe they felt they had found a replacement for Frank Gardner.

When Milo announced closing Clint invited the two men to the bar for a last drink, on him. . . .

". . . was another fella we were playin' with for a while," Lehane said, "a real good card player, like you, name of Frank Gardner. Know him?"

"I've heard of him," Clint said. "I heard he was real good. I don't think I'm in his class, though."

"Real close," Lehane said, gesturing with his beer so that some of it slopped over onto his arm. He didn't seem to notice. "*Real* close, am I right, Coban?"

"Real close," Coban said. "You gonna be around tomorrow to play some more, Clint?"

"I probably will," Clint said. "Too bad Gardner left, though. I'd sure like to play against him. You boys wouldn't happen to know where he went, would you?"

"Where he went?" Lehane asked. "We didn't even know he was leavin' until he was gone."

"Without so much as a by-your-leave," Coban said mournfully.

Clint was going to have to remember to say good-bye to these two when he left. They seemed to have really had their feelings hurt by Gardner's abrupt departure.

TEN

Clint sat in his room and read the telegrams again. The only positive thing he'd accomplished that day was to have Ben Thompson and Rick Hartman working for him, trying to find Frank Gardner. The doctor had not been very helpful, and all he'd managed to find out from Coban and Lehane was that they actually *enjoyed* losing money to better poker players than they were.

The only person there was left to question was the saloon girl, Darla. Up close he had found her to be very pretty, and there was some intelligence in her eyes, as well. This only served to leave him even more impressed by Frank Gardner. It wasn't only twenty-one-year-old girls, sixty-year-old doctors starved for some intelligent conversation, and a couple of bad poker players he had managed to win over. This was a grown woman whom, he was sure, had been around and heard a lot of lines from a lot of men.

Tomorrow he'd have to track her down during the day and see what she knew.

He had pulled off his boots and hung his gun belt on the bedpost when there was a knock at the door. He took the gun from the holster, walked to the door, and opened it just enough to see who was there. He wasn't going to have to track Darla down tomorrow afternoon after all. Here she was standing outside his door.

He opened the door wide, holding the gun behind his back. She was still wearing the dress she'd worn at the saloon, very low-cut, revealing acres of white cleavage but through a shawl she had thrown over it. Somehow, the effect was even more enticing.

"Hello, Darla," he said. "Kind of late to come visiting, isn't it?"

"That depends on what your definition of visiting is," she said. "May I come in?"

"Well, sure."

He backed away, let her enter, then closed the door and walked to the bedpost. He replaced the gun in the holster and then turned to face her. She had taken the shawl off and tossed it away. Her breasts were large and firm and smooth, and there was a deep, dark valley between them.

"Wait a minute," he said. "Did Milo send you over here?"

"No," she said, "he doesn't know I'm here."

"Then to what do I owe the pleasure?" he asked.

She pouted a moment and said, "I thought we were sending signals to each other tonight. Was I wrong?"

"Well, no, you weren't wrong . . ."

"Don't you find me . . . attractive?"

"Hell, yes, you're beautiful."

She moved closer to him and asked, "Then you don't want me to leave?"

"Well, no—"

"You want me to stay, don't you?"

Before he could answer she pulled his head down to her so she could kiss him, her tongue flicking across his lips with a featherlight touch.

"I'm not a prostitute," she said, "in case you were worrying about paying me."

"Well, no . . ."

"Then kiss me."

This time he gathered her into his arms and kissed her soundly, bringing a moan from deep in her throat just before her tongue plunged into his mouth.

"It's even better when you help," she said breathlessly.

She backed away from him, reached behind her, and undid a clasp or something. The top of her dress fell away and her breasts leaped into view.

"You are beautiful," he said.

"Show me," she said, "enjoy me . . ."

He reached for her breasts, palmed them, hefted their weight, thumbed the nipples, then helped her get the dress the rest of the way off. He ended up on his knees in front of her, pressed his mouth to her soft belly, licking the smooth skin, tonguing her navel, reaching behind her to cup her ass.

"Mmmm," she said dreamily as he continued to kiss her belly and then worked his way down even further. Her pubic hair tickled his nose as he poked in it with his tongue, looking for her. When he found her she jumped, backed up a bit until the back of her legs struck the bed. She sat down, then lay down and opened her legs to him. He slid his hands beneath her and lifted her so he could get at her with his mouth.

"Oh, God," she said. "Oh, Jesus, yes . . . right there . . . ooh, oooh, oooooh . . ."

He slid his tongue in and out of her, then up and down the length of her wet slit until he found that hard little nub hiding beneath some skin. He used the tip of his tongue to liberate it, then flick it back and forth, then just roll his tongue over it and finally just suck it between his lips . . . and she went crazy. She started to buck and writhe and gush all over his mouth and face. He lapped at her, enjoying the sharp, tangy taste of her, and kept at it until she reached down to push his head away.

"God," she said, "you've got to let me breathe!"

"Okay," he said, getting on the bed with her, "but only for a little while."

ELEVEN

Her energy amazed him. They had sex at the four corners of the bed, and then right in the center of it with her on her hands and knees, her rump pressed firmly up against his belly. When he exploded inside of her he did so with a loud bellow, and then he had no strength left in his legs. He fell forward on top of her, pinning her to the bed, his penis still twitching inside of her.

"I like feeling your weight," she said.

"I'm sorry," he said, moving.

"No, it's fine," she said. "I said I liked it."

He still felt badly about falling on her like that. He slid out of her, and then lay down next to her. She remained on her belly, and he ran his palm over the smooth globes of her butt.

"You're amazing," he said.

"Well," she said, "I had to pay you back after what you did to me—and for me—the first time. I don't think a man has ever made me feel that way."

"Not even Frank Gardner?"

She hesitated, then said, "W-what?"

"Come on, Darla," he said. "This has been a lot of fun, but didn't you come up here because you heard me talking about Gardner in the saloon?"

Her head was facing away from him, and now she turned to look at him. The look on her face was sheepish.

"How did you know?"

He smiled. "I know when I'm sending signals to a woman," he said, "and when she's sending them to me—and we just weren't, tonight."

She took a deep breath and then said, "Well, if I knew then what I know now, I would have."

"So would I," he said. He leaned over and kissed her left buttocks tenderly. "But the truth is, we're both looking for information about Frank Gardner."

"How did you know that?" she asked, surprised.

"Well, I was going to try to find out from you tomorrow where he is," he said, "but you beat me to it. You came up here hoping to find out from me, right?"

"Now you're amazing," she said. "That's just what I was trying to do."

"So you have no idea where he went?"

"None."

"And you were seeing him while he was here?"

"Oh, yes," she said, "we were . . . well, doing this. But now that I think of it, he didn't do it as well as you do."

He took that remark with a grain of salt.

"Did you know he was seeing Beatrice Haskell, too?"

"Oh, I knew about her," she said, "I don't think she knew about me—but I think she found out."

"Why do you think that?"

"I think that's why she made him leave town."

"*She* made *him* leave town?"

"I believe so."

"Everybody else thinks he ran off with her."

"Her father thinks that," Darla said. "He thinks she's his little girl. He doesn't know what a little bitch she was."

"Fathers never seem to know that about their daughters," he said.

"And they don't want to."

He lay down on his back and put his hands behind his head.

"So I guess we're both just wasting our time here, huh? We're not going to get anything out of each other about Frank Gardner."

"Well," she said, sliding her hand over his belly now, "maybe not about Frank Gardner . . . but I don't really think we're wasting our time . . . do you?"

She took hold of his penis and began to stroke it, and as it swelled in her hand he had to agree with her. They weren't wasting any time at all.

TWELVE

In the morning they spent some more time not wasting time and Clint got dressed while she watched—although he would have preferred it the other way around.

"How much longer will you be in town?" she asked.

"I'm not sure," he said. "A day or two, maybe, until I get a line on Frank Gardner."

He strapped on his gun last, then looked at her.

"When I find him do you want me to tell you where he is?"

"You know," she said, "if you had asked me that last night I would have said yes."

"But not now?"

"No, not now," she said. "You've shown me that there are real men out there. I know that I won't wake up to-morrow and find you gone, unless you've said good-bye. I won't have to wonder where you are or what happened, which is what I've been wondering about him for months— but not anymore."

"Good," he said. "You're much too much woman to be worried about a man like Frank Gardner."

He went to the door, then turned around.

"You can stay as long as you like," he said, "and come back when you like."

"Just between you and me," she said, "I hope you don't locate him for a long time. It's selfish, I know, but there it is."

"Hey," he said, "we're all entitled to be a little selfish sometimes. Right now I'm going to go and have breakfast. That's me being selfish."

"I'll see you later, Clint."

"Bet on it" he said and left the room.

Over breakfast he decided to give it one more day in El Paso. If he didn't have word from Ben Thompson or Rick Hartman by tonight, then he would send them another message each telling them that he was on the move. Darla was a great lady, but he didn't want to take a chance on her getting too attached to him. He didn't want any feelings of guilt when he left.

Once he left town, though, the question would be in what direction to go. Where would a man like Frank Gardner go to ply his trade? A boomtown like Leadville or a city like Denver or San Francisco? It seemed like he had made his fair share of friends in town, but didn't tell any of them what his plans were.

Unless one of them was lying.

His top candidate for liar was Doc Owens. He thought the man knew more than he was saying, but how could he get it out of him?

Over his second pot of coffee he looked up and saw Keith Abel enter the dining room. It still hadn't come to him where he'd seen Abel's father before. He was wondering if he was going to have to start avoiding the man.

"Hey, Clint," Abel said, approaching the table, "glad I caught you."

"Sit down, Keith," Clint said. "Have some coffee."

Abel sat down and poured himself a cup.

"What are you doing in town again so soon?"

"The boss sent me," the other man said. "He's real

anxious to know if you found out anything yet.''

"Well, I've found out some things, but not where Gardner and Beatrice are.''

"What'd you find out?''

"Nothing that would do him any good to know,'' Clint said. "Just tell him I'm still working on it.''

"Oh . . . well, okay, sure,'' Abel said. "What about what, uh, we talked about?''

"I'm sorry, Keith,'' Clint said, "but it still hasn't come to me where I met your father. Believe me, when it does I'll let you know.''

"Ah, I know you will,'' Abel said. "I've just got to stop bothering you about it. It'll come to you.''

"I'm sure it will.''

Abel pushed away the untouched cup of coffee and said, "I've got to run some errands and get back to the ranch.'' He stood up. "I'll tell the boss what you said.''

"Okay, Keith. See ya.''

Keith nodded and left the dining room. Clint wondered what reason he'd given Haskell for coming to town. He doubted the old man had sent him. As much as Haskell wanted to know where his daughter was, he wouldn't be *that* impatient.

Finishing his coffee he spotted a copy of the local newspaper, the *El Paso Ledger*, on a nearby table. He reached over, picked it up, and scanned the first page. It looked like they picked stories up from other papers, but there were a couple of local stories there, which gave him an idea. Back when Gardner was shot, and shot two men, it must have made the newspaper. Maybe somebody from the paper had talked to the gambler, and maybe he'd let something slip about where he'd be headed next.

He looked at the paper for the name of the editor and the location of the paper. When he paid the waiter he asked him where the newspaper office was and got directions.

"You want to place an ad?'' the man asked.

"Not really," Clint said. "I'm just looking for some information."

"Well," the waiter said, "a newspaper is where you usually get it."

Clint hoped the man was right.

THIRTEEN

Clint found the newspaper office, a small, cluttered, noisy storefront that reminded him of many others he'd been in. He could smell the paper and the ink, and of course the man who turned to face him was covered with black dirt/ink.

"Are you David Conrad?" Clint asked. "The editor?"

The man shook his head and pointed toward the back of the room. That was when Clint noticed that there *was* another room, with a closed door separating it. He walked to the door and knocked. He thought he heard someone say, "Come in," but he couldn't be sure with the noise of the press.

He went in anyway. A man was sitting at a cluttered rolltop desk.

"What is it?"

"Are you David Conrad?"

The man turned and looked at him.

"That's right." He was in his thirties, medium build, with thinning brown hair. "What can I do for you?"

"You're the editor of the paper?"

"Editor, reporter, and, if that young fella out there doesn't get it together, I'll be typesetting and running the press, as well—not that I haven't done it all before." The

47

man frowned at him. "You don't want to buy an ad, do you?"

"I'm afraid not."

"I didn't think so. I don't recognize you, so you're not a merchant here in town."

"I'm passing through."

"And you wanted to look at the newspaper office?" the man asked.

"I'd like to ask you some questions."

"About what?"

"About something that happened here some time back."

"How far back?"

"Actually," Clint said, "I'm not sure. There was a shooting over a poker game, two men were killed—"

"And Frank Gardner was wounded," Conrad said. "I remember. Why are you interested in that?"

"I'd like to find out where Gardner went when he left here."

"Why, you want to shoot him, too?"

"No," Clint said, "I just want to find him."

"Why?"

"A friend of mine asked me to."

"Who?"

"Howard Haskell."

"Ah, now I get it," Conrad said, standing up. "You're a detective who Haskell hired to find his daughter. Would you submit to an interview—"

"No."

The man frowned.

"No interview, or no, you're not a detective?"

"Both."

"Then what—"

"I'm just a friend of Howard who he asked for help," Clint explained.

The man studied Clint for a few moments and then asked, "So, as a friend, do you have a name?"

Clint hesitated, because he knew what would happen

when he told the man his name. It happened every time he ran into a newspaperman, without exception. Maybe, he thought, it won't happen this time.

"Clint Adams."

The man's eyes widened and Clint thought, So much for that.

"The Gunsmith?"

"Look—"

"Jesus," he said, looking around for something to write with, something to write on, "would you do an interview—"

"I said no interview."

Conrad stared at him.

"But that was before I knew who you were."

"That's okay," Clint said, "I knew who I was, and the answer is no."

"So you won't do an interview, but you want me to help you."

"That's it, exactly."

"You've got a lot of nerve."

"Not really," Clint said. "Look, I just want to know if you interviewed Gardner after the shooting."

"If I answer—"

"No interview," Clint said, "but Howard Haskell will be very grateful to you."

Conrad thought about that for a while, then raised his eyebrows and nodded.

"What do you want to know?"

"Did you interview him?"

"I tried to get a comment from him."

"And?"

"He wouldn't talk to me. He was kinda abrupt . . . like you."

"He was, huh?" This was no help, at all. "Well, thanks, anyway."

"Wait a minute," Conrad said. "You can't just walk out without answering a question or two."

Clint faced the man and said, "This is not an interview."

"No."

"I won't be quoted in your newspaper."

Conrad made a face and said, "Not if you don't want to be."

"I don't."

"All right."

"Okay, then," Clint said, "ask your questions."

"How long have you been in town?"

"Since yesterday."

"How long will you be staying?"

"Until tomorrow."

"That's all?"

"That's it."

"Have you gotten anybody mad at you while you've been in town?"

"If you're hoping there'll be some trouble while I'm here, forget it," Clint said. "I'll be leaving in the morning, and nobody's mad at me. I'm afraid nobody will be getting shot for your newspaper."

"Well, you said something about Howard Haskell being grateful to me."

"You didn't tell me anything I could use."

"Hey, I answered your questions," Conrad said. "I cooperated."

"Well . . . I'll tell him that. He's a wealthy man. It won't hurt to have him feeling kindly toward you."

"No, it won't," Conrad said. "So what's your next move? How are you gonna find out where Gardner took Haskell's daughter?"

"I don't know," Clint said. "I'm just going to have to keep looking, I guess."

"And you're sure you won't do an interview?"

"I'm positive."

"Well, I'm sorry to hear that."

"Look, Mr. Conrad, thanks for talking to me."

"Sure," Conrad said, "what the hell. It's not like anybody reads the damn newspaper, anyway."

Clint refused to feel sorry for the man. The only times he'd ever agreed to newspaper interviews they came out all wrong. He didn't think this fellow would be any different.

"Well, thanks again," he said and left, walking through the other room to the front door, but unable to do so without wincing from the noise. He didn't know how anybody could work all day long around a printing press.

After Clint Adams left his office David Conrad went out to the man running the press and tapped him on the shoulder. Immediately the noise died down.

"Yes, sir?"

"Ned, I'm going out for a while. If anybody's looking for me, you don't know where I am."

"What are you gonna be doing?" Ned asked.

David Conrad smiled and said, "I'm going out looking for trouble."

FOURTEEN

After Clint left the newspaper office he felt like he was at a dead end. Maybe he should just mount up and ride out of El Paso today—but where would he go? Maybe that was the question he should be asking himself. Where would he go if he were Frank Gardner, and he had a young, beautiful girl with him who probably hadn't ever seen anything other than El Paso and her father's ranch?

New York?

Boston?

San Francisco?

Europe?

No, not the last. A gambler wouldn't spend the money it would take to get to Europe, not when he could gamble it. It was more likely they went someplace in the United States. Maybe someplace like New Orleans or Denver. Someplace where he could gamble, and where she would be impressed.

There were too many places in addition to the ones he'd already thought of. Philadelphia, Washington, D.C., Sacramento, a young girl would be awed by all of them.

He had to pass the telegraph office so he stopped in to see if he'd received any other telegrams. The clerk shook his head and apologized.

"Nothing else, sir."

"Thanks, anyway."

He left the telegraph office and started down the street. He saw a man coming his way, walking very purposefully and wearing a badge. Usually, when he got to a town he checked in with the local law, but he'd been a little preoccupied since arriving in El Paso.

It seemed as though the local law was coming to him, though.

"Clint Adams?" the man asked.

"That's right, Sheriff," Clint said. "What can I do for you?"

The lawman had close-set eyes, and he narrowed them now as he glared at Clint.

"I'm Sheriff Crown," the man said, "and I don't appreciate you comin' into my town without lettin' me know, Adams."

"You're right, Sheriff," Clint said. "I apologize."

The man hesitated, then said, "What?"

"I said I'm sorry. I'm here doing a favor for my friend, Howard Haskell, and it just slipped my mind. I should have come to see you."

"You're friends with Mr. Haskell?"

"That's right," Clint said. "He's asked me to try and find his daughter."

"She left town with that gambler, Frank Gardner."

"I know that," Clint said, "but I don't know where they went."

The sheriff suddenly looked around them, then back at Clint.

"Why don't we talk in my office," he suggested.

"Sure, Sheriff."

"I just put on a fresh pot of coffee when Conrad came running in."

"Conrad? The newspaper editor?"

"That's right," the sheriff said. "He came running into my office to ask me if I knew the Gunsmith was in town."

"I see."

"I don't mind tellin' you it riled me having him tell me how to do my job."

"I guess so," Clint said, as they walked toward the man's office. "I guess I've got to apologize to you for that, too."

"No," Crown said, "you can stop apologizing. You've done it enough."

"Then why are we going to your office?"

"To talk about Frank Gardner and Beatrice Haskell," Crown said, "which I don't want to do on the street."

"Do you know something—"

"I might know something helpful," Crown said, "but why don't we wait until we get to my office. All right?"

"That's fine with me, Sheriff," Clint said.

FIFTEEN

As they entered the office, Crown asked, "Do you like strong coffee?"

"That's the only kind I like."

"Have a seat."

Crown retrieved two cups of coffee from a pot on the stove in the corner and brought them back to his desk. Clint was looking around the office, which looked sort of unusual.

"Used to be a café," Crown said, handing him a cup of coffee, "that's why I have a real stove."

"I see. I thought it looked a little odd."

"Real cells in the back, though," the man said proudly. "Imported from back east."

This was not the office Dallas Stoudenmire had had when he was in El Paso—but then, Stoudenmire had been the marshal, not the sheriff.

"What's on your mind, Sheriff?"

"I know Beatrice Haskell, Adams," he said. "I've known her for years, watched her grow up."

"And?"

"I don't like the way Gardner whisked her away."

"My understanding was that she went willingly."

"He convinced her that she wanted to go willingly,"

57

Crown said. "That's the kind of man he was."

"How well did you know Gardner, Sheriff?"

"Not before he came to town," Crown said. "We talked when he first arrived, and then didn't speak in earnest until he gunned down two men over a poker game. Did you hear about that?"

"I heard it happened," Clint said. "I understood they thought he was cheating."

"They called him a cheater," Crown said, "and he gunned them down."

"Didn't they have guns?" Clint asked.

"Sure, but they never had a chance."

"Did you arrest Gardner?"

"I wanted to," he said, "but I couldn't."

"Why not?"

"Everyone in the saloon backed his story."

"Which was?"

"That they called him a cheat and drew first."

"Which made it self-defense."

"Sure," Crown said.

Clint wondered how well Crown knew Beatrice, and if there was some jealousy at work here.

"Sheriff, do you have any idea where Gardner may have gone with Beatrice?"

"Beatrice always talked about going places, Adams," Crown said. "Boston, New York . . . Paris."

All places that Clint had already thought of.

"Which one do you think they went to?"

"I don't know," Crown said, "but mark my word, they went someplace big."

Again, Clint had already figured that out. He finished the coffee—which wasn't all that good—and set the empty cup on the lawman's desk.

"Do you have anything else for me, Sheriff?"

"Hmm? Oh, no," Crown said, "that was it."

Clint stood up.

"Well, I'm obliged for the information."

"How much longer will you be in town?"

"I'll be leaving tomorrow," Clint said, "just ahead of trouble, unless your newspaper editor has his way. He must be running around town telling people I'm here, hoping somebody will come gunning for me."

"That would be his style," Crown said.

"If I shoot him," Clint said, "you'll know why, huh, Sheriff?"

"You'd be doin' me a favor. If you don't shoot him, though, I'll be having a word with him about this. The last thing I need in town is a newspaper editor who tries to manufacture trouble."

Clint waved and left the office. Crown had had very little in the way of useful information, so Clint was still at a dead end in El Paso.

What he needed was a nice fat telegram, chock-full of information.

SIXTEEN

That night Clint played poker again with Coban and Lehane, and two others. For bad poker players they were extraordinarily lucky, and so outlasted the other two. Once again it became a three-handed game late into the night, until Milo called it to a halt.

Clint felt badly about taking their money, and so he bought them drinks again.

"I'll be leaving in the morning," he told them.

"That's too bad," Coban said. "We've enjoyed playing poker with you."

"You have to forgive me for asking this, of both of you," Clint said.

"You don't have to ask," Lehane said. "You want to know why we bother playing when we play badly and lose?"

"Yes."

He shrugged and said, "We enjoy it."

"And we don't mind losing because it's how we learn," Coban said.

"Maybe," Lehane said, "we won't be so bad forever."

"Just remember," Clint said, "you don't need to see the last card to know that you don't have the winning hand."

The two men exchanged a look and then Coban said, "You make it sound so simple."

They left, leaving Clint with Milo.

"You didn't find out what you wanted," Milo said.

"No," Clint said, "but it's not here to find out, so I'll have to look elsewhere."

"Where?"

"I don't know, Milo," Clint said. "I don't know . . . yet."

Clint went to his room and found Darla waiting there for him.

"You're leaving tomorrow, aren't you?" she asked from his bed.

"Yes."

"Then come to me," she said, opening her arms. The sheet fell away, revealing her full, firm breasts, the nipples already hard with desire and excitement. "These will be two nights I never expected to have. I'll remember them forever."

"So will I," Clint said, discarding his clothes and moving into the warmth of her embrace.

SEVENTEEN

Clint woke the next morning and, not in any particular hurry to leave, dallied with Darla even more. They had enjoyed each other throughout the night, falling asleep in each other's arms, waking to enjoy again, then sleeping. He woke that morning curiously rested for all the energy they'd expended together. Later he'd realize that if he had slept the night alone he would not have been there to receive the information when he did.

He was dressed, watched again by her, when there was a knock on the door. When he opened it the clerk from the telegraph office was there.

"This came first thing when I opened the office," he said, handing Clint a telegram.

"Thank you," Clint said, accepting it.

"What is it?" Darla asked.

"A telegram from a friend," he said, "telling me where Frank Gardner is."

"Really?"

"Yes." He read the telegram again, then folded it and put it away. He looked at her. "Do you want me to tell you where he is?"

She hesitated a moment, then smiled and said, "No. I don't need to know."

He kissed her and said, "Good girl."

"Stop in here if you ever pass near to us in the future," she said.

"I will," he said, "I promise."

He left El Paso and rode to the Haskell ranch. He left Duke out front, as he wasn't staying, and knocked on the door. He was surprised when it was opened by Howard Haskell, himself.

"Have you heard anything?" the older man asked.

"I've heard they might be in San Francisco," he said, touching Rick Hartman's telegram through his shirt.

"Not for sure?"

"No," Clint said. "My friend says only that he's heard that Gardner was there. He may not be there now or when I get there."

"But you're going?"

"Yes, I am," Clint said. "When I know for sure, Howard, I'll send you a telegram."

Haskell grabbed Clint's arm and squeezed it.

"I'm grateful, Clint, truly."

"I know you are," Clint said. "I'll find her, Howard."

He went back down the steps and mounted up. As he rode Duke away from the house, he saw that he was going to have to pass Keith Abel, who was walking toward him. He could have kept going, but he chose to stop.

"Have you gotten a line on them?" Abel asked.

"I might have," Clint said. "I'm going to check it out."

"But . . . we'll hear from you, won't we?"

"Oh, yes," Clint said. "When I find Beatrice I'll let Howard know."

"That's good."

"And when I remember where I saw your father," Clint added, "I'll let you know, Keith."

"I didn't want to ask . . ."

"I won't forget," Clint said. "I promise."

"It's just that . . . well . . . it's important . . ." Abel stammered.

"I know it is, Keith," Clint said. "I know."

Clint was going to use the journey from El Paso to San Francisco to search his brain, his memories, and try to come up with Keith Abel's father.

EIGHTEEN

San Francisco

Frank Gardner stared across the poker table at the man everyone called Diamond Jack Vincent. Gardner couldn't see where the man had gotten his name. There wasn't a diamond on him, and he hadn't bothered to ask during the introductions.

There were five men in the game, which was being played in a private room in the back of the St. Charles Gambling House in Portsmouth Square.

Gardner had not heard of any of the gentlemen he was playing against, but that was okay, because they had never heard of him, either. He had been playing poker throughout the West for several years, but this was his first time in San Francisco. It had taken all this time for him to save up enough of a stake to come to Portsmouth Square and play against the best—and so far, he'd been acquitting himself quite well. In fact, he'd been very happy since arriving in San Francisco. Once he let it be known that he had enough money to buy into a private game, the cards had been falling his way, he loved the hotels and restaurants, and there was a never-ending stream of willing ladies. The only sour note in the whole experience was having Beatrice Haskell along.

In El Paso bringing Beatrice had seemed like a good idea. For one thing, she had money, a small inheritance left her from her mother. She'd been able to get that out of the bank before her father could stop her. With that added to what he'd already saved, he had enough to come to San Francisco—but he had to bring her with him.

Of course, having her as his "girlfriend"—as she put it—had not stopped him from seeing other women in El Paso, so it certainly didn't stop him from seeing them in San Francisco. Of late, however, Beatrice had begun to bitch and moan and act the shrew every time he left the hotel room. He told her to go out and shop or do whatever she wanted to do, but she insisted she hated San Francisco. How anyone could hate this city was beyond him, but he was convinced that the young woman was simply afraid of the big city. She was, after all, only twenty-one, and had never been outside of El Paso. More than once, however, he had suggested she go back there, but she insisted she was going to stay with him because she loved him.

Love had never entered into the equation for Frank Gardner, unless it was the love of a good card game, good food, good liquor, or a loose woman—for the moment.

Diamond Jack Vincent looked back at Gardner and smiled.

"I believe it's your bet, Mr. Gardner," the man said, in what Gardner felt sure was a manufactured Southern accent.

They each had four cards on the table, one down, three up. Gardner's three up cards were a queen of hearts, a queen of spades, and a king of clubs. Diamond Jack had a nine and ten of diamonds, and a queen of diamonds.

Gardner looked twice. Maybe there was a reason the man was called "Diamond" Jack, after all.

"One hundred," Gardner said.

"You put a lot of faith in queens, my friend," Diamond Jack said, "especially when I have one of them."

"That's the bet," Gardner said.

"Well," Diamond Jack said, "in that case I'll call the hundred and raise three hundred."

He was raising on a possible straight flush. Even if he had a matching card underneath—an eight, jack, or king of diamonds—he was still only betting on four cards. Gardner already had the winning hand on the table, a pair of queens. A high pair was usually formidable in a game of five-card stud.

"Call the bet," Gardner said, and tossed in three hundred dollars worth of chips.

"Cards," the house dealer said, and dealt each of them their last card.

"Well, well," Diamond Jack said, "look at that, a diamond jack. That's usually a lucky card for me."

"A possible straight flush," the dealer called, "needs a king or an eight."

He dealt Gardner's card, and it was a king of hearts.

"Two pair on the table," the dealer said.

"Ooh," Diamond Jack said, smiling, "that's the kind of hand that can cost you a lot of money, my friend."

"Or win a lot," Gardner said, "and my name is Gardner, not friend."

"Sorry," Diamond Jack said, "just trying to be friendly."

Diamond Jack was smooth. His skin was very smooth, making him look ten years younger than his thirty-five years. His hair was smooth, combed straight back from his forehead and slicked with something shiny. His suit, his movements, they were all smooth.

"Two pair bets," the dealer said, putting the deck of cards on the table for the last time.

Gardner stared across at the up and down straight flush on the table in front of Diamond Jack. There was no way the man wasn't going to play it like he had it, not with that last card actually *being* a diamond jack.

That was the kind of card that had probably cost him a lot of money in the past . . . or won a lot.

"Five hundred," Gardner said.

"Well, well," Diamond Jack said, "that's confidence for you."

"Five hundred to you, Mr. Vincent," the dealer said.

Vincent frowned, just slightly, but Gardner caught the tiny little wrinkle between his eyebrows, and knew that he had him.

"There's no way you'd fold this hand, is there?" he asked Gardner, who just stared at him. "Ah, well," Diamond Jack Vincent said, "I'll call."

"Your bet is called, Mr. Gardner."

Gardner turned over his hole card. It was the king of diamonds, giving him a full house. It was also the card that would have given Diamond Jack his straight flush. The other card—the eight of diamonds—had already been folded earlier in the game by another player. Gardner remembered that.

Vincent sighed, turned over his hole card, which was an eight of clubs. He had a straight, which would have beat the two pair on the table, if that was all Frank Gardner had had.

"Full house wins," the dealer said, "and, gentlemen, that ends the game. The house wishes to thank all of you for playing."

Diamond Jack sat forward and extended his hand across the table to Gardner.

"Well played, Mr. Gardner."

Gardner hesitated only a moment before accepting the man's handshake.

"And you, Mr. Vincent."

"That diamond jack usually is a lucky card for me, you know," he said to Gardner.

"In this case," Gardner said, "I guess the diamond king would have been even luckier."

NINETEEN

San Francisco was one of Clint's favorite cities. When he wanted to get away from trail dust and boomtowns, he either went there or Denver or New York.

He usually stayed at one of the smaller hotels just outside of Portsmouth Square. They were still comfortable and still had gambling, but they were not as crowded or expensive as the hotels in the Square, like the Alhambra or the El Dorado.

This time he chose a place called the Black Ace Hotel and Gambling Hall, which he'd never been to. He didn't want to be recognized right away, just in case Frank Gardner and Beatrice Haskell had somehow heard that he was looking for them.

He knew that a man named Case Dilman owned the Black Ace. He'd heard the story from Bat Masterson. Dilman called it the Black Ace because he'd made his first fortune in a poker game when he caught the black ace he was looking for to fill out his hand. When Clint asked Bat why the man called it the Black Ace and not the Ace of Spades or the Ace of Clubs, Bat said that Dilman couldn't remember which one it was. Clint didn't know whether he believed the story or not, but maybe he'd get a chance to ask Case Dilman himself—if they had occasion to meet.

He checked in, taking just a moment to examine the lobby. If it had been decorated to Dilman's taste, then the man's taste was rather understated. While small, the hotel could still have been fashioned after some of the Portsmouth Square establishments, but that didn't seem to concern Dilman. There was no crystal and no overstuffed chairs. The public was not encouraged to sit in the lobby and read a newspaper. Rather, they were encouraged to enjoy their rooms or enjoy the gambling.

Clint liked it. When he went up to his room to drop off his gear, he found he liked *it* as well. The Black Ace had a nice, intimate feel that appealed to him.

He wondered if the place would appeal to a man like Frank Gardner, or if Gardner would prefer the allure of the Portsmouth Square hotels and halls. He was betting on the latter. The only way to find Gardner was going to be to start at one end of the Square and work his way to the other. Before leaving Howard Haskell's ranch he had managed to get a photograph of Beatrice from him. Wealthy people usually took lots of photographs of their families, and of the things they owned. Sometimes, they were one and the same.

He took the photograph from his saddlebag and stared at it. There was no doubt that Beatrice had grown up to be quite lovely, but to Clint she still looked like a young girl. Of course, this picture only showed her from the neck up. She might have also had other attributes with which to attract a man, but for now Clint wondered if the main attraction for Frank Gardner had not been money.

He replaced the photograph. He didn't need to carry it with him to recognize Beatrice Haskell. To him she looked almost the same as she had when he had last seen her.

From the neck up, anyway.

TWENTY

Beatrice looked up from the bed when Frank Gardner entered their suite at the St. Charles.

"Finally," she said.

"Don't start, Bea," Gardner said.

She made a face and tried to keep from retorting. She knew she was turning into a nag. What she wanted to avoid was turning into a shrew, but it wasn't easy when you lived with a man who had very little regard for your needs.

"Did you win?"

"Of course I won," he replied.

Why was she waiting for the day he'd come back and say no, that he had lost? Why did she think that maybe that would change things between them? Maybe, if he lost, he'd need her?

"What took so long?" she asked, unable to keep it from coming out.

"That man I beat in the last hand wanted to buy me a drink," he said.

"Who was that?"

"His name is Diamond Jack Vincent."

"Was he the good-looking one?" she asked.

Now it was his turn to frown as he removed his jacket and unbuttoned his shirt cuffs.

"I don't know if he's good-looking," he said, untying his tie and tossing it aside.

"The smooth-looking one," she said. "Was he the smooth-looking one?"

"I guess you could say he was smooth-looking," Gardner said. "I didn't realize you looked so hard at other men."

She smiled sweetly and said, "Not as hard as you look at other women." If only it stopped at looking!

"Are we going to start that again?" Gardner asked.

God, she thought, how she loved when that slight Southern accent showed up in his tone. He hated it, hated it in his own voice and hated it when other people tried to affect it. He grew up in New Orleans, in the bayou, and hated that, too.

"No," she said, "we are not. Can we go get something to eat?"

He stared at her, his shirt unbuttoned so that she could see his hairy chest. She loved wrapping that hair around her fingers, and he hated it when she did it.

She stared at him, unable to help loving him. He had thick black hair, smooth skin, full, sensuous lips that she loved to kiss, and that she *loved* feeling run all over her body. If only the sex with him wasn't so wonderful, if only she could find a flaw . . . but not considering her feelings, wasn't that a flaw? One that she could use to convince herself to leave him?

"Bea, I'm tired," he said. "I just finished eighteen hours of poker. Can't you go down and get yourself something to eat?"

"Sure, I can," she said, getting up off the bed. She'd been lying on it fully dressed, waiting for him to come back and take her to dinner. "Or maybe I'll find some man who'd like to buy me dinner."

He ignored her.

"Like maybe Diamond Jack Vincent?"

He looked at her and smiled. It infuriated her how sure

he was of her, of her love for him. Sometimes she thought she should sleep with another man just to shake his confidence.

"Why not?" he asked. "I think he's down in the dining room right now, as a matter of fact."

"You know," she said softly, approaching him, running her hand through the hair on his chest, "sometimes you can be a real bastard!" As she said "bastard" she wrapped her hand in his chest hair and pulled!

"Ow, goddamn it!" he shouted, as she ran for the door. "You know how I hate that, Bea!"

"Yes," she said, "I do know," and she ran out the door.

As she walked down the hall to the stairway she wondered if there was any way she could stop herself from loving Frank Gardner.

TWENTY-ONE

Clint had dinner that evening in his hotel. This was his practice when he stayed in a new place, to sample the food right away. He ordered a steak and vegetables, and it came with a basket of hot, freshly baked biscuits. He had a huge mug of cold beer with it, then topped it off with a pot of strong coffee and a slice of peach pie.

"Was everything to your satisfaction, sir?" the waiter asked.

"Yes," Clint said, "everything was wonderful. Could you charge this to my room, please? It's room—"

"No, no, sir," the waiter said, "this meal is on the house."

"Oh, really?" Clint said. "And what did I do to deserve that?"

"Compliments of the owner, sir."

"The owner?"

The middle-aged waiter nodded, then inclined his head toward a corner of the room.

"Mr. Dilman, sir," he said.

Clint turned and saw a man sitting alone at a corner table, with one of the huge mugs of beer in front of him. He lifted it and held it up in a silent salute.

"Mr. Adams," the waiter said, "Mr. Dilman would like

to know if you would join him for a drink?''

"Tell him I'd be happy—no, never mind," Clint said, rising. "I'll tell him myself. Thank you."

"Yes, sir."

Clint walked across the room to Dilman's table, and the man stood to greet him.

"Mr. Adams," Dilman said, "such a pleasure to have you staying with us. Can I offer you something?"

The two men shook hands and Clint said, "Another one of those beers would be fine."

Dilman held his mug up and nodded to the waiter.

"Please," Dilman said, "join me."

Clint hesitated, because, of the three chairs available, none of them offered a view of the entire room. While he hadn't been able to get a corner table for dinner, he had managed to get one against the wall.

"Oh," Dilman said suddenly, "of course. Excuse me. I'm in your seat."

The man stood up and moved to one of the other chairs, taking his beer with him.

"Thanks," Clint said, taking the vacated chair. "I know it must seem silly, but—"

"Not at all," Dilman said. "I know there have been times when I, myself, have felt much safer with my back to the wall."

Clint took a moment to study his host. He appeared to be in his late thirties, not tall, not thin, however, not average. His suit certainly wasn't average, and a star sapphire ring glittered on the middle finger of his right hand—although Clint didn't know what kind of stone it was, at the time.

"You must check your register each day to see who checks in," Clint commented as the waiter brought Clint's beer and gingerly set it down in front of him.

"I keep an eye on things, yes," Dilman said.

"And do you treat all your new guests to a free meal?" Clint asked.

"Hardly," Dilman said with a laugh, "only those I want to meet or have mutual friends with."

"And we have mutual friends?"

"We do," Dilman said. "Bat Masterson, for one."

Even though it had been Masterson from whom Clint had first heard about Dilman and his black ace, he didn't recall Bat saying they were friends. Maybe this was a case of one man considering the other a friend, and the feeling not being returned. Clint had been on the wrong end of those kinds of friendships before.

"Is that a fact?" Clint said. "You know, it was Bat who told me your black ace story."

"Oh," Dilman said, "that."

"It's not true?"

"Oh, it's true, all right," Dilman said. "I'm just always embarrassed that I can't remember what suit the card was."

"Well, I guess it doesn't much matter," Clint said. "It was a winning hand."

"Actually," Dilman said, shifting in his chair, "it wasn't."

"What?"

"I mean, I *won* the hand, but I didn't have the winning hand. See, the game was five-card stud, and the ace fell last."

"And you bluffed with it?"

Dilman nodded.

"You want to tell me who the other player was? The one you bluffed?"

"I don't think so."

"Just his initials?"

Dilman laughed.

"I don't think it would be fair."

"Well, what did you have?"

"I had aces over, but the man thought I had aces full."

"And what did he have?"

"Kings full."

"Whoa," Clint said. "Did you . . ."

"No," Dilman said, "he didn't pay, so I didn't let him see the cards."

"Don't know if I could have passed that up," Clint said, "I would have *had* to see them."

"Then you wouldn't have been bluffed out," Dilman said.

"Well," Clint said, raising his beer, "here's to the black ace."

TWENTY-TWO

Clint and Dilman talked a bit longer and then the man asked Clint why he was staying at the Black Ace, and why he was in town.

"Well, as to the Black Ace," Clint said, "I've just never stayed here before. I'd heard about it, so I decided to try it."

"And we're glad you did," Dilman said. "Now, why are you in San Francisco? Not looking for a high-stakes poker game by any chance, are you?"

"Not this trip," Clint said. "I'm here looking for a man and a woman—a young woman."

"What's her name?"

"Beatrice Haskell," Clint said. "She's the daughter of a friend of mine from Texas."

"Not Howard Haskell?"

"Well, yes, it is Howard. How did you know?"

"I make it my business to know the names of most of the wealthy men in the country," Dilman said. "You know, just in case their names appear on the register."

"Well, apparently his daughter took off with a gambler, and my information has it that the man is here in San Francisco."

"Staying where?"

81

"That I don't know."

"Can you tell me his name?"

"That I can tell you," Clint said. "It's Frank Gardner."

Dilman thought a moment, then shook his head and said, "It doesn't ring any bells with me, but I tell you what I can do. I can put out some feelers around the city. Maybe he's in a high-stakes game somewhere."

"I'd appreciate it," Clint said. "I've been told he's a good poker player, but my sources are rather suspect. I don't know what level of play he's used to."

"Well, if it's high stakes," Dilman said, "the level of play really wouldn't matter much, as long as he had the money."

"Well, the girl has some money," Clint said, "but I'm not sure how much."

"I guess Howard Haskell's daughter might have enough to do it," Dilman said. "Is that why you figure he took her with him? The money? Is she . . . well, homely?"

"No, actually she's very lovely."

"And young?"

"Twenty-one, I believe."

"Well," Dilman said, "that's young, but it's not that young."

"Young enough," Clint said. "I understand Gardner is—well, around your age."

"Well, then, twenty-one isn't that young," Dilman said with a smile. "I've seen girls that age, myself."

"You've seen girls that age from San Francisco, I'm sure," Clint said. "Beatrice had never been out of El Paso, until now."

"I see. Well, I wish you luck in finding them. I'll do what I can to help."

"I appreciate it."

"What are you going to do the rest of tonight?" Dilman asked.

"I thought I'd start hitting the hotels in Portsmouth

Square,'' Clint said. ''I thought I might get lucky and spot him.''

''Well,'' Dilman said, ''I hope you'll have time to give our little establishment a try before you leave. I'm really quite proud of it.''

''I'm sure I will have time,'' Clint said, standing up. ''And thanks for the drink and the meal. I hope you're going to let me pay the rest of the time I'm here.''

''Oh,'' Dilman said, ''I think I'll insist on it. Have a good evening.''

''And the same to you,'' Clint said, and he left the dining room of the Black Ace Hotel, quite impressed with its owner.

TWENTY-THREE

Beatrice recognized Diamond Jack Vincent because Gardner had pointed the man out to her one day in the lobby of the St. Charles Hotel. She saw him in the dining room, sitting alone at a table, eating his dinner. She decided to be bold and try to make Gardner jealous. She entered the dining room, and when the maître d' asked if he could seat her she said, "I'm dining with that gentleman over there."

"Mr. Vincent?"

"Yes."

"Follow me, please."

She followed him to Diamond Jack's table.

"Mr. Vincent? Your dinner guest has arrived," the man said to the gambler.

To Vincent's credit he didn't miss a trick.

"Well, thank you, Henry. I'm afraid she's so late I started eating without her."

"I will have Albert come right over and get her order," Henry said.

"Thank you," Vincent said.

Henry held Beatrice's chair and then walked away when she was seated.

"If we made a dinner date," he said to her, "and I forgot, I should be shot."

"I'm afraid I'm the one who should be shot, Mr. Vincent," she said. "I simply didn't want to eat alone, so I lied to the gentleman about dining with you. Thank you for not giving me away."

"My dear," Vincent said, "any man who would give you away is a fool."

"Well," she said, "I guess you have a way with words and cards."

Albert, the waiter, appeared then and took Beatrice's order. Vincent told him to make sure the chef rushed it, but still cooked it correctly.

"I'll see that it's taken care of, sir," Albert promised.

"Thank you, Albert."

As the waiter left, Vincent looked across at Beatrice and asked, "Should I know you?"

"I don't think so," she said. "My name is Beatrice Haskell."

"And what are you doing in San Francisco, Beatrice Haskell?" he asked. "I haven't seen you in any of the casinos."

"I haven't been in any of them," she said. "I don't gamble."

"What do you do?"

"Not much, really," she said. "Sometimes I shop."

"And is that what you came here to do? Shop?"

Beatrice wondered at that point if she should tell Vincent about Gardner.

"To tell you the truth," she said, "I'm not sure what I came here to do."

"Ah," he said, as if he understood.

"What do you mean by 'ah'?" she asked.

"You came here with a man."

"How did you know?"

"The only time a woman admits she doesn't know what she's doing is when she's involved with a man."

"And are you speaking from experience?" she asked. "As a man who has been involved with many women?"

"Well, of course," he said, smiling and making a magnanimous gesture with his hands. "Can't you tell by looking at me that I've had experiences with many women?"

"I suppose I can."

He leaned forward and added, "And perhaps I'll add you to the list."

"You consider dinner an experience?"

"With a girl as beautiful as you are?" he asked, sitting back in his chair. "Definitely."

"Well," she said, "I can definitely believe that you've been with a lot of women. You sure know how to talk to them."

She found Vincent to be completely charming during the meal, totally attentive. Even when other women walked past their table—beautiful women—he paid them no mind. She thought that Frank could take some pointers from him. His head swiveled around to look at other women constantly when they were together.

Vincent waited for her to finish her meal so they could have dessert together, and when the meal was over he told Albert to put it on his room bill.

"Oh, no," she said, as the waiter walked away, "I didn't mean for you to pay for my dinner—"

"But I am," he said, "and that's that. I'll be going into the casino now. May I escort you there?"

"Oh, I don't think I should," she said. Being seen with him in the dining room was one thing, but being seen on his arm in a casino was another entirely. "I think I'd better go to my room," she said.

"Well, then," he said, standing, "I'll escort you to the lobby."

He pulled her chair out for her, and they walked to the lobby together.

"Thank you for dinner," she said when they got there. "I had a very enjoyable time."

"As did I," he said, "and you tell Frank Gardner I think he's a fool to let you roam about alone."

"Fran—you knew?"

He smiled, took her hand, and kissed it.

"I saw you in the lobby the same day you saw me," he said. "I hope to see you again, Miss Haskell."

"I hope to see you, too, Mr. Vincent," she said.

He turned and walked into the casino. She watched him until he was gone, and then turned to go up the stairs. She wondered if she was going to have the nerve to tell Frank Gardner what she had done.

TWENTY-FOUR

Clint prowled Portsmouth Square until the small hours of the morning and didn't spot anyone resembling Beatrice Haskell. He saw quite a few men who matched Frank Gardner's description, but none of them were him.

He returned to the Black Ace while there was still time to do some gambling, as he had promised Case Dilman he would do so. As Clint entered the casino section of the hotel, Dilman spotted him and came over.

"Any luck with your search?"

"Not tonight."

"I don't have any information yet," Dilman said, "but I'm working on it."

"That's okay. I didn't expect anything to happen this quickly."

"Well," Dilman said, standing next to Clint and surveying the casino, "what do you think of my little place?"

"It's not so little," Clint said. Whatever money Dilman had saved on the lobby of the hotel he'd spent here. The Black Ace Casino was a smaller version of many of the Portsmouth Square gambling halls. "In fact, it's very impressive, Case."

"Thanks," Dilman said. "That means a lot coming from you."

"Me? I'm no expert on casinos."

"You've gambled in the best," Dilman said, "and, from what I've heard, you've gambled with the best."

"Meaning Bat Masterson and Luke Short," Clint said. "They're my friends and are kind enough to allow me to play poker with them. I'm not in their league."

"That's not what Bat tells me."

"Really?" Clint said. "That's funny, it's what he tells me."

"Right before you and he are going to sit down at the same table, no doubt."

"Well, seriously," Clint said, "I think this place is great, Case. I think I see an opening at a roulette wheel."

"Roulette?" Dilman asked.

"What's wrong with roulette?"

"It doesn't strike me as your kind of game," Dilman said. "Where's the thought processes involved?"

"In what number you pick."

"That's what I mean," Dilman said. "It's just picking a number."

"And knowing how much to bet on it."

"Most people just keep putting the same amount of money on a number, waiting for it to hit."

"Well, I don't play the same number all the time," Clint said. "Then there really is no thought involved. Sometimes I play some of the other bets: black or red, odds or even, a section of the board."

"You're cutting your odds when you do that."

"And increasing your chances of winning."

"I still can't see you at roulette," Dilman said, shaking his head. "Now blackjack, there's a game."

"Jesus," Clint said, "a lot of time for very little return."

"That depends on how much you bet."

"I don't like the game enough to bet big at it," Clint said.

"Faro?"

"I've played it," Clint admitted, "and dealt it. It's not my game."

"Poker, then."

"Not in a casino game," Clint said.

"Why not?"

"Too much going on around the table. Too many people, too easy to cheat."

"I have spotters in the room."

"A good cheater can fool a spotter."

"Are you saying you could cheat and my spotters wouldn't catch you?"

"Not me," Clint said hurriedly. "I'm not a magician with a deck of cards, but some people are."

"Would you care to make a little wager?"

"What kind of wager?"

"You bring somebody in and have them cheat," Dilman said, "and my spotter will spot them."

"And if he doesn't?"

"You win a thousand dollars in chips to cash in or gamble with, as you see fit."

"And if you win?"

Dilman thought a moment, then said, "You deal faro for me for a week."

"Room and board?"

"Of course."

"It's a bet," Clint said, and they shook hands.

"Who are you planning on bringing in?" Dilman asked.

"Ah, that would be telling."

"I know all the card sharps in town, Clint."

"Then I'll have to bring someone in you don't know. What's the time limit on this bet?"

"It has to be resolved before you leave San Francisco," Dilman said.

"Okay, then," Clint said, "I might as well check out your house dealers and see who the easiest ones to cheat on will be."

"My dealers are the best," Case Dilman said.

Clint grinned and said, "We'll see, won't we?"

TWENTY-FIVE

When Beatrice awoke the next morning, Gardner was kissing her belly. She moaned and reached for his head, but it scooted lower and then he was between her legs, his tongue doing marvelous things to her, things no other man had ever done.

Who was she kidding? She'd only had one lover before Gardner, and he was a local boy who just wanted to pull it out, put it in her, and finish. He never took time with her the way Gardner did. The gambler treated her breasts like they were dessert, sucking and licking them, biting the nipples, spending more time on them than Beatrice had ever thought possible. The first time he'd gone between her legs with his mouth, she thought she was going to die. She never thought she'd feel anything so good—and then he entered her, and took her to even newer heights.

She stared down at the top of his head. His ass was up in the air, and it was beautiful. In fact, he was a beautiful man, a man women wanted, and she knew that he wanted women, beautiful women. She was flattered, at first, that he wanted her, and then she got possessive. She used to scream and shout when he looked at other women, but she quickly realized that if she wanted to be with him, if she wanted moments like this, she was going to have to put up with all of that.

Suddenly, his tongue swirled around her, entered her, and then he was on top of her, inside of her, and all other thoughts simply fled. . . .

"Don't you want to know where I had dinner last night?" she asked later.

They hadn't talked about it when she returned to the room. They'd made love hurriedly, and then he had fallen asleep. She thought that perhaps this morning's slower, more thoughtful lovemaking was payback for that.

"I assume you ate in the hotel dining room," he said, tucking in his shirt and then reaching for his tie. He stood in front of the mirror to tie it, and she saw that he was looking at her reflection. "I keep telling you to try other places, to get out of this hotel, but you insist on doing everything here."

"It's . . . very big out there," she said in a small voice. "There are so many people."

He finished with his tie and reached for his jacket, then turned to face her.

"Most of them aren't so bad, Bea," he said. "If you tried meeting new people, talking to them, you'd understand that."

"Aren't you afraid?" she asked.

"Afraid of what?"

"That if I meet other people I might meet some other man."

"Who'll take you away from me?" he asked, laughing. He came to the bed and kissed her, a long, slow kiss during which his tongue made just a fleeting appearance in her mouth. She was immediately wet and ready again . . . and then he backed away.

"I don't think so," he said.

"Bastard!"

He laughed again.

"Do you want to come down and have breakfast with me today?"

"No," she said. "I'm not ready—I need a bath. It would take me too long to get ready."

"All right, then," he said. "I'll see you later."

"What are you going to do?" she asked.

"What I always do," he said, halfway out the door. "Find another game."

Another game, she wondered, or another woman? She rolled over in bed, pressed her face to the pillow, and cried softly.

TWENTY-SIX

Clint rolled over in bed and bumped into somebody. He opened his eyes and looked at the woman next to him. They had met in the casino last night, late, too late for much conversation. Their eyes met, there was a spark, and then she was in his room, naked in his bed.

She was apparently a sound sleeper. His bumping into her did not awaken her. It occurred to him suddenly that they had tumbled into bed together so fast that it had not dawned on him that she might be a professional. Was she going to expect money this morning? He had never paid for sex before, and he wasn't about to start now.

He tried to remember her name but couldn't. He remembered her ass, though. It was heart-shaped, smooth, and firm, and it was facing him now as she was curled up on the edge of the bed. The cover sheet had long since been kicked from the bed during a frenzied session where his legs had become tangled in it.

He sat up in bed and studied her from behind. She was full-bodied, there was no escaping that. He liked a roll of flesh here and there on a woman, rather than a woman who was flat as a board in the belly or flanks. There was nothing flat about . . .

What was her name?

He couldn't very well wake her up without first remembering her name. Of course, being there in bed with her, with her butt so close, and the smell of her in the air, he had begun to swell, and his erection was rather insistent at the moment.

He reached out and ran a hand over her behind, enjoying the smooth feel of her warm skin. He straddled both cheeks with his hand, running his middle finger along that deep crease between them. She moaned and moved, pressing back against his touch. He moved closer to her, replacing his middle finger in that delicious crack with his penis. He reached around to the front of her, grazed her breasts with his palm, then ran it down over her belly until it was between her legs. She moaned again, spreading her legs for him. He touched her, stroked her until she was wet, then slid his penis between her heavy thighs and up into her.

"Oooh, God," she said, "what a way to wake up, mmmmm . . ."

He began moving in her, and she met each of his thrusts by pressing her butt back into him. He slid his finger along her crease, stroking her while he fucked her from behind, and she began to gasp for air as their thrusts became faster and harder. . . .

He slid his right arm beneath her, leaving his left draped over her so that he was able to touch her with both hands, explore her body at the same time that he moved in and out of her. Her curves were opulent, her breasts large and, while perhaps not as firm as they once were, still lush and exquisitely pleasant to touch and knead. Her nipples were large, almost like grapes, her thighs heavy and smooth. She was a luscious woman and her appetite for sex had awakened him more than once during the night. Now he was returning the favor in the morning.

Her movements became frenzied, as they had when the sheet was kicked off the bed, and he knew he had to rush if he was going to keep up with her. As it turned out he didn't quite make it, but that was fine. She was in the throes of her own passion when his overtook him, and he exploded inside of her, causing her to gasp and catch her breath, and causing him to yell out loud. . . .

"Eileen," she said moments later.

He was still lying spooned up against her, still inside of her, in fact.

"What?"

She turned her head so she could look at him. She had lots of dark hair and some lines at the corners of her dark eyes and her lush mouth. He never objected to that sort of thing on women. It only added to their beauty, and that was the case here.

"Eileen," she said. "It's my name. I wanted to save you from the embarrassment of trying to remember."

"I would have," he said, "after I regained my senses."

She took his left hand in hers and raised it so she could tongue his fingers, suck on his thumb.

"You have great hands, Mr. Clint Adams," she said. "You really know how to use them on a woman."

"I try," he said.

"Lots of experience, I bet," she said, still holding his hand but now pushing it down between her thighs. "You know, all I had in mind last night was some gambling— until we saw each other."

"As I recall," he said, "there were several men gathered around you, making you offers of one kind or another."

"Ah," she said, "but the silent offer I received from your look across the room, that was the one I responded to, wasn't it?"

"Was I making an offer?"

"I thought you were," she said. "If not, then perhaps I've forced myself on you."

"No, no," he said, "I don't believe that's the case, at all."

"No," she said, laughing softly, "neither do I. Well, what do we do now?"

"What do you mean?"

"I could get up and get dressed and leave, and that would be that. Of course, I don't know how Case Dilman would like having a disheveled-looking woman wandering across his lobby."

"You know Dilman?"

"Of course," she said. "I know most of the men who run these gambling halls. I gamble quite a bit, you see, and—to their delight—badly. But to get back to the subject at hand . . ."

"Which is?"

"How to avoid the awkwardness of the morning after," she said.

"I don't feel awkward," he said. "Do you?"

She settled back against him and sighed.

"You know," she replied, "I really don't, and it surprises me."

"So there's no reason for either of us to get up just yet," he said, wriggling the fingers of his left hand, which was still trapped between her thighs, "is there?"

"No," she said, "I suppose there isn't."

She turned, suddenly, using her weight to push him onto his back.

"It's my turn, though."

"To do what?"

She took his penis in her hand, her thumb on the swollen head, and said, "To wake you up."

He groaned as she stroked the length of his penis.

"At this rate," he said, "I'll never regain my senses. . . ."

TWENTY-SEVEN

When Clint finally did regain his senses he was ravenously hungry. Eileen declined his invitation to breakfast.

"When you have a body like mine," she said, "you have to be careful what you put into it."

"There's nothing wrong with your body that I can see," he said.

"You're sweet," she said. "Now get out of here so I can get myself together."

He went down to the dining room for a steak and egg breakfast and to collect his thoughts. The first thing he had to do today was to send telegrams to Ben Thompson and Rick Hartman and let them know where he was staying. Also, the same for Howard Haskell. After that, he'd have to start wandering Portsmouth Square again, unless Case Dilman had come up with a piece of information.

Speak of the devil, Clint thought, as Dilman showed up during his second pot of coffee.

"You're looking content this morning," Dilman said. "Mind if I join you?"

"Please do."

Dilman sat and poured himself a cup of coffee.

"Did you have a pleasant night?"

"Very pleasant," Clint said. "Why do I get the feeling you know who I spent it with?"

"I know lots of things," Dilman said. "I saw you and Eileen meet last night. She's a nice lady. Gambles a little too much, but she's got the money for it."

"How much money?"

"She's got a line of credit at every casino in the Square," Dilman said, "and then some."

"That's a lot of money."

"But she's not a happy woman," Dilman said.

"Why do I now get the feeling you know her real well?" Clint asked.

"Knew her," Dilman said, "a long time ago. Now we're acquaintances of long standing."

"I see," Clint replied, "so you have no problem with me . . ."

"Oh, no," Dilman said, "no problem at all."

He was either a very good poker player, or he was telling the truth.

Clint chose to believe the former. He liked to think he knew when somebody was bluffing.

After breakfast Clint went to the nearest telegraph office to send his messages to Ben Thompson and Rick Hartman. He had to wait because there were several men ahead of him. Most of them were sending telegrams to someone asking them to send money. What they didn't tell the person at the other end was that they had lost all of theirs in Portsmouth Square and would probably lose whatever that person sent them, as well.

Clint wondered about people who gambled and lost all the time. He enjoyed gambling, but he didn't enjoy losing. If he lost all the time he would never gamble just to gamble. Winning was the best defense against becoming a loser, Bat Masterson had once told him. Bat seemed to be able to win most of the time at will. Sometimes, with him, it didn't even seem to be gambling.

Bat claimed that he wasn't gambling when he played poker, he was playing poker. If he wanted to gamble then he'd spin the roulette wheel or play faro or he'd throw dice. He was in control when he was playing poker, and that kept it from being gambling. Clint knew that Luke Short felt the same way. He wondered how Case Dilman felt.

By the time it was his turn to send his telegrams he had them all written out. He gave them to the clerk, paid him, and told him where he was staying.

"Sure thing, Mr. Adams," the clerk said. "Soon as an answer comes I'll have someone run it right over."

"Thanks a lot."

He left the telegraph office and walked to Portsmouth Square. He began cruising the hotels and gaming palaces again.

The last place he stopped that afternoon was the St. Charles.

It took Beatrice a long time to get ready, and when she left the hotel room it was closer to lunchtime than breakfast. When she got down to the lobby she thought she saw someone she knew going into the casino. She couldn't be sure because she hadn't seen him in so long. She was excited, though, at the prospect of maybe talking with someone she knew, so she crossed the lobby and entered the casino.

The man was standing right in front of her, just looking the place over. Timidly, she stepped forward and tapped him on the shoulder.

Clint turned and was surprised to see Beatrice Haskell standing there.

"Clint?" she asked. "Clint Adams?"

In an instant Clint made his decision on how to play it with her.

"Beatrice?" he asked. "No, it can't be."

"It is."

"Beatrice . . . Haskell?"

She immediately threw her arms around him and hugged him tightly. Clint had only seen her picture from the neck up and now that she was pressed tightly against him he could see why a man like Frank Gardner would be attracted to her—beyond her money.

"It's been years!" she said, holding him tightly.

"I can't believe it," he said, holding her at arm's length. "Look at you, all grown up. The last time I saw you, you must have been ten years old."

"Eleven," she said. "I'm twenty-one now."

"Twenty-one," he said, shaking his head, hoping he wasn't overdoing the act. "I can't believe it. What are you doing in San Francisco? Is your father with you?"

"I was about to have some lunch," she said. "Please come with me. We can catch up."

"You have a date," he said, taking her arm and putting it through his. "Let's go."

TWENTY-EIGHT

Over lunch she bombarded him with questions about the things he'd done over the past ten years, the things she'd heard he had done. She never let up and made it almost impossible for him to ask her any questions. Finally, he just had to force it.

"So tell me, how's your father?"

She looked away for a moment and said, "He's fine."

"Is something wrong?"

She looked somewhere else again, and then finally right at him.

"Well, the truth is . . . we're not speaking to each other."

"Oh," he said, "I'm sorry to hear that. That must be tough on your father. He loves you very much."

She had the good sense to look guilty as he said that.

"How long has this been going on?"

"It's been months," she said.

"Well, then, are you in San Francisco alone? Have you moved here?"

"No, I haven't moved here . . . and I'm not alone. You see, that's the problem."

"What is?"

"I'm here with a man . . . a man my father doesn't approve of."

"Oh, I think I see," Clint said. "Can I ask who the man is?"

"Maybe you've heard of him," she said. "His name is Frank Gardner."

She was being very honest with him, which made him feel bad for deceiving her about why he was really there. Also, it was obvious from the way she was talking that she had no idea that her father had sent him to find her. He had thought that word might have gotten back to Gardner.

"I don't think I have heard of him," Clint said. "What does he do?"

"He . . . plays poker."

"A professional poker player?"

She nodded.

"That's something else your father probably didn't approve of."

"You're right."

"Well . . . he must be good at it if he does it for a living. Uh, can I ask . . . how old he is?"

She gave him a small smile and said, "That's something else my father doesn't approve of."

"Ah, he's older than you."

She nodded.

"A lot older?"

She nodded again, then said, "He's almost your age."

"Thanks a lot."

"Oh, I'm sorry," she said, "I just meant—"

He laughed and said, "It's all right. I know what you meant. Well, do you love him?"

"Very much."

"And he loves you?"

"I . . . think he does, yes."

"You think?"

"Well, he says he does."

"And you don't believe him?"

"Well . . . we haven't been together all that long."

"You're not married, are you?"

"No."

"Well, where is he? Can I meet him?"

"He's out, right now. He just finished a high-stakes poker game, which he won, and he's out looking for another game."

"Oh, yes," he said, "there's always another game."

"You sound disapproving," she said. "Don't you play cards?"

"Not for a living," he said, "and when I win I don't look to invest it into another game."

"Well, that's what he does because that's how he wants to make his living."

Clint reached across and covered her hand with his.

"You don't have to defend him to me, Bea."

"Thank you, Clint," she said. Then she made it hard on him and asked, "You won't tell my father you saw me, will you?"

"Does he know where you are?"

"No, and I don't want him to."

"Well," he said, "I don't think I'll be talking to your father anytime soon."

He didn't technically "lie" to her.

TWENTY-NINE

Once she told Clint about her father and Frank Gardner, she suddenly seemed ready to unburden herself to him.

"It's just very hard living with a man who gambles for a living, I guess," she said. "It's his first love, you know?"

"I do know, Bea," he said. "I have a lot of friends who are gamblers."

"That's why I thought you'd understand, and maybe you'd be able to advise me."

Thinking about Darla, back in El Paso, Clint said, "Well, there's another problem with gamblers, you know."

"What's that?"

He watched her face carefully as he said, "Most of them are womanizers."

There was just a flash of pain across her face before she quickly covered it.

"Is that another part of the problem, Bea?" he asked pointedly.

"To tell you the truth, Clint, I'm not sure," she said. "He does look at other women, but I really don't know if it goes beyond looking."

"Why don't you ask him?"

"I can't."

"Why not?"

"He'd say I was accusing him."

"Are you afraid he'd leave you?"

She bit her lip and nodded.

"And if he did that, what would you do?"

"I'd die," she said, and he found it to be a little girl's answer.

"I don't think you'd die, Bea."

"I'd be stranded here."

"Don't you have money of your own?"

"Well . . . yes, of course I do."

Clint was sure she wasn't being entirely truthful, there.

"So if he left you, you could go back home."

"Oh," she said, covering her face with one hand, "I couldn't!"

"Why not? Wouldn't your father take you back?"

"I'm sure he would," she said, "but I just couldn't go back there, Clint. I'd be disgraced."

"Are you afraid of what they'd say in town?" Clint asked.

She nodded, then added, "Not about me, but about my father. I shouldn't have said I'd be disgraced, I should have said I've disgraced him."

"He'd take you back in a minute."

"You haven't seen him in ten years," she said, "but you're right, he would. The simple fact of the matter is I don't want to go back to El Paso. If Frank left me I'd just stay here and . . . and get a job. Make the best of it."

"Why would you have to get a job? You said you had money."

"I do," she said, "but it wouldn't last forever."

"Bea," Clint asked, "is Gardner gambling with your money?"

"It's not like that," she said, quickly going on the defensive. "We put our money . . . together. . . ." she said lamely.

"But you had more than he did, didn't you?"

"Well . . . yes . . . Clint, he didn't just take me with him for my money."

"I never said he did."

"But you're thinking it, and that's not it," she said. "I'm sure of it."

"Good," he said, "I'm glad you're sure."

There was an awkward silence then, and Clint took the opportunity to call the waiter over and ask for the check.

"No," she said, "I can have it charged to the room."

"That's okay," Clint said, "I'd like to buy you lunch, Bea."

"All right."

He paid and they left the dining room.

"Have you seen anything of San Francisco?" he asked.

"Not really," she said. "Frank tells me to go out but . . ."

"You don't want to go alone."

"Right."

"Would you like me to show you around?"

"No," she said, "that's okay. You're probably here on business—"

"Not really," he said. "I come to San Francisco every so often just to enjoy the city. You should at least see the rest of Portsmouth Square."

At that moment Beatrice recognized another familiar face across the lobby, this one of much more recent acquaintance.

"That's all right, Clint," she said. "I do plan to see the rest of it."

"Do you have someone to show it to you?"

"I have someone in mind," she said.

"Well, good. Uh, you'll be in town awhile, right?"

She nodded.

"Frank says there are a lot of games to play here. We'll be here for quite a while."

"Well, good," he said. "Then I'll stop by the hotel and see you again before I leave."

"I'd like that very much," she said, kissing him on the cheek. "It was nice to see you again, Clint. Thanks for listening."

"It was my pleasure," he said, once again feeling guilty.

THIRTY

Clint's first thought was to go back to the telegraph office and send a telegram to Howard Haskell telling him that he'd found Beatrice. Instead, however, he went back to his hotel to think about it.

He went into the hotel bar, got a beer, and took it to a corner table. Briefly, he wondered what it would be like to have a life where you didn't have to worry about what table you sat at.

He was halfway finished with his beer when Case Dilman entered, saw him, and came over.

"I've located your Frank Gardner," he said with satisfaction.

Clint decided to play along and not tell him that he'd already found him.

"Where is he?"

"He's staying at the St. Charles," Dilman said, sitting across from Clint. "He just finished a high-stakes poker game."

"How did he do?"

"Word is he won."

"He must be pretty good, then."

"Not really," Dilman said. "From what I heard there

113

was only one other player in the game who was really good.''

''Who was that?''

''Diamond Jack Vincent.''

''I've heard of him,'' Clint said. ''He is supposed to be pretty good.''

''That's what I've heard,'' Dilman said. ''Gardner may or may not be good, though. You know anybody can get lucky.''

''I know it,'' Clint said. ''Is the girl with him?''

''That I don't know,'' Dilman said. ''I can have someone go over and look, though.''

''No, thanks,'' Clint said, ''I can do that myself. You've done enough. Thanks, Case.''

''I'm glad to help, Clint,'' Dilman said.

''Have a beer?''

''Later,'' Dilman said. ''I still have a hotel to run.''

''Okay, then I'll see you later,'' Clint said, ''and thanks again.''

''Sure.''

As Dilman left, Clint was left with his same question. Should he tell Haskell his daughter was in San Francisco with Frank Gardner? Why not? Wasn't that what he was supposed to do, what he'd promised to do?

Why did he feel so guilty about it, then? Maybe he should have just told Beatrice the truth, but that might have sent her and Gardner packing.

Or maybe just one of them?

After Clint left Beatrice in the lobby of the St. Charles, Diamond Jack Vincent came walking over to her.

''Friend of yours?'' he asked.

''An old friend.''

He laughed.

''You're not old enough to have 'old' friends,'' he said.

''A friend of my father, then,'' she said. ''We just ran

into each other. He offered to show me around Portsmouth Square.''

''And did you take him up on the offer?''

''No.''

''Why not?''

''Because I thought I might get a better offer.''

''From who?''

''From you, Mr. Vincent—that is, unless you have something better to do.''

''Isn't Frank going to show you around?''

''I don't think so,'' she said, ''and I don't want to wander around by myself. I might end up getting lost.''

''Well,'' Jack Vincent said. ''We couldn't have that, could we?''

He stuck out his arm and she linked hers through it.

THIRTY-ONE

Frank Gardner rolled over in bed, found his watch, and checked the time.

"You have an appointment?" the woman next to him asked.

"I have to get back," he said.

The woman sat up. She was a blowsy-looking blonde with startling blue eyes and just the hint of a double chin. The sheet fell away from her full, almost chubby but firm breasts.

"Afraid your little rich girl will miss you?" she asked.

"There's no point in looking for trouble," he said, tossing back the sheet.

Before he could get up, she reached her hand into his crotch and took hold of him.

"Sara—" he said, but she tightened her hold.

"It seems to me," she said, "that you'd be looking for trouble if you tried to leave me right now."

"Sara—" he said, softer this time. He turned toward her and ran his hand over her.

"That's better," she said as he slid his hand down between her thighs. He leaned over and began to kiss her breasts, sucking the nipples until they were as hard as pebbles.

"Mmmmm," she said, then pushed him away with surprising strength. "Can your little rich girl do this for you?"

She pushed him onto his back, then leaned over him and took his rigid penis into her mouth. He marveled at how she could take the entire length of him in, her nose nestling in his pubic hair. The answer to her question was no, Beatrice never did this. The only time he'd approached her about it she had reacted with shock that he would expect her to do such a thing. She thought it was dirty.

Sara Tinsdale had no such problem. She was happily sucking him now, riding him up and down with her talented mouth. They had met in one of the casinos a few days after he and Beatrice had arrived. He didn't remember which one, but it didn't matter. They had almost immediately ended up in her room, and since then he had been seeing her two or three times a week, when he could get away.

Now that the high-stakes game he was in was over, it was easier for him to slip away under the pretense of "looking for another game." The truth of the matter was he already had another game lined up. It was to begin in two nights, but that gave him two days worth of sneaking away to be with Sara, who was older and more experienced than Beatrice in the ways to please a man.

Like the way she was pleasing him right now.

THIRTY-TWO

Clint was waiting for Beatrice in the St. Charles lobby when she walked in. When she spotted him she was glad that Jack Vincent had left her off in front of the hotel because he had business elsewhere. She wouldn't want to have to explain him to Clint.

"I didn't expect to see you again so soon," she said.

"Can we get a drink?" he asked. "I have something to tell you."

"It sounds serious."

"Let's wait until we're having that drink," he said. He led the way into the hotel bar. It was afternoon and it wasn't busy. He left her at a corner table and went to get their drinks. She said beer would be fine, so he returned with two.

"Now what's so important?" she asked.

"I haven't been completely honest with you, Bea."

"About what?"

"About why I'm here."

There was an awkward moment of silence, and then she sat back in her chair, shoulders slumped.

"My father sent you, didn't he?"

He nodded. "He asked me to look for you."

"And you found me," she said. "Boy, he asked the right man, didn't he?"

"Bea—"

"Have you told him yet that I'm here? With Frank? Is he on his way?"

"No to all of those."

"Why not?"

"I felt bad about lying to you," he said. "I wanted to tell you the truth first."

"What makes you think I won't run again?" she asked.

He shrugged and looked down.

"Oh, I get it," she said. "I understand. You think I'll tell Frank and *he'll* run. That would make everything easier, wouldn't it?"

"Do you think he will?"

"No, I don't."

"He'd face your father?"

"He's not afraid of my father, Clint," she said. "It was my idea to leave El Paso and not tell him where we were going, not Frank's."

"I see."

"No, you don't see," she said. "You don't know at all what kind of man he is."

"Maybe I'm about to find out."

"What?"

"Am I mistaken," he asked "or did he just walk in?"

She turned and looked over her shoulder.

"That's him," she said.

When Frank Gardner entered the bar he wasn't looking for Beatrice, but there she was, sitting with a man. Was she trying to make him jealous? He smiled, waved, and walked over to them.

"Introduce me to your friend, Bea," Gardner said.

"Frank," she said, "this is an old friend of my father . . ."

"Nice to meet you," Gardner said, extending his hand.

". . . Clint Adams," Bea finished.

Gardner's hand faltered, but he regrouped and completed the handshake.

"I guess I'd better sit down," he said.

"Frank, my father asked Clint to find us."

"Well," Gardner said, taking a seat, "he is an important man if he can get the Gunsmith to run his errands for him."

"It's not an errand," Clint said, "it's a favor for a friend. Maybe that's something you know nothing about."

"I have friends, Mr. Adams."

"I hope so, Mr. Gardner," Clint said, "because you might need them."

"Is that a threat?"

"I'm not here to threaten you," Clint said. "I was just letting Bea know that I'll be sending her father a telegram today telling him that the two of you are here. I'm sure he'll be on the first train."

"I see," Gardner said, folding his arms. "You're expecting me to run before he gets here, is that it? That's the kind of man you think I am?"

"I don't know what kind of man you are, Gardner," Clint said, standing up, "but I guess we're about to find out. Bea, again, I'm sorry. I guess you'll both just do what you have to do."

With that Clint left the St. Charles bar.

"Wow," Gardner said, letting out a breath. "The Gunsmith, huh?"

"Yes," she said. "I haven't seen him since I was eleven. I thought I found him this afternoon, but I guess it was the other way around."

"What do you want to do, Bea?"

"Do you want to leave San Francisco, Frank?" she asked her lover.

"No," he said. "I have another game set up two nights from now. I'm not about to walk out on that."

"And me?" she asked. "Do you want to walk out on me?"

"Bea," he said, taking her hand, "when your father gets here we'll face him together. That's the way I wanted it in El Paso, remember? Running away was your idea."

"I know it was."

"So now that they've found us," he said, "we'll do things my way. All right?"

"All right, Frank," she said, "we'll do it your way."

THIRTY-THREE

Clint went from the St. Charles Hotel to the telegraph office and sent a telegram to Howard Haskell saying that he had found Gardner and Bea.

"Funny you should come in now," the clerk said. "I was just gonna send a boy over to your hotel. You got a telegram, too."

"Well, then, I'll save him the trip," Clint said. He accepted the telegram and then sent his. He stepped outside before reading his. It was from Rick Hartman and had some very interesting news. Apparently, Frank Gardner's real name was Frank Gleason. He had changed it somewhere along the way, and one of Hartman's contacts in San Francisco knew about it. The end of the message gave Clint the contact's name, in case he wanted more information.

He did.

By coincidence—which Clint usually hated—the contact was a man he knew, a private detective he'd met the last time he was in San Francisco. His name was Dominick Polo. Clint remembered that Polo's office was on Market Street and decided to go directly there.

"Well, Mr. Adams," Polo said as Clint entered his office. "It's nice to see you again. What brings you here this time?

123

Last time you were referred by our mutual friend Talbot Roper.''

"Apparently, you get around, Mr. Polo," Clint said. "This time you were referred to me by our mutual friend Rick Hartman."

He still had the same dark hair and the same air of competence about him.

"Well, then, I guess that means we both get around," Polo said. "Does this concern the information I gave Rick about Frank Gardner?"

"Yes, that his real name was Gleason?"

"That's right. Why don't you have a seat."

The office was cramped, and was made more so by standing up.

"What can I do for you?"

"Well, I'd like to know why Gleason changed his name to Gardner."

"It has to do with something that happened in his past," Polo said. "He hasn't been Gleason for a long time."

"What was it that happened?"

"Well, apparently during a poker game a man was accused of cheating and was taken outside and beaten to death."

"What did Gleason—or Gardner—have to do with it?"

"He was one of the players."

"Wait a minute," Clint said, sensing another coincidence. "When did this happen?"

"About twenty years ago."

"Where?"

"Caldwell, Kansas."

"And was the accused cheater named Jack Abel?"

"That's right," Polo said. "You knew him?"

"I met him once, and I've been trying to remember where," Clint said, "but this . . . this is too much of a coincidence."

"What's so coincidental about it?"

Clint told Polo that he was in town on behalf of his friend

Howard Haskell, and that Haskell's foreman's name was Keith Abel.

"As in Jack Abel?"

"His son."

"That is a coincidence," Polo said.

"Do you know if Gardner—or Gleason—was actually one of the men who beat Abel to death?"

"That I don't know," Polo said. "All I know is that he was there, and he changed his name afterward."

"Well, that would be an indication of guilt, wouldn't it?" Clint asked. "What happened to the men who beat Abel to death? Were they arrested?"

"This was twenty years ago, Clint," Polo said. "That was sort of frontier justice, I guess, like hanging a horse thief on the spot."

"I guess so," Clint said. "Do you know the names of the other players?"

"A couple," Polo said. He wrote down two names and passed the paper over to Clint, who read it and didn't recognize them. "Are they involved, too?"

"No," Clint said, tucking the paper away, "I never heard of them."

"Is there anything else I can do for you?" Polo asked.

"Not right now, Dominick," Clint said, "but I'd like to keep my options open."

Both men stood and shook hands.

"What do I owe you?" Clint asked.

"For conversation? Nothing."

"What about the work you did finding all this out?" Clint asked.

"I'm billing Rick for that," Polo said. "If you want to settle with someone, settle with him."

"Okay," Clint said. "I'll do that."

Polo walked him to the door and said, "Maybe we can get together before you leave town. You know, for dinner or something."

"Sure, I'd like that," Clint said. "Do you gamble?"

''All the time,'' Polo said, ''but not the kind you're referring to.''

''Okay, then dinner. I'll be in touch.''

Clint left, armed with information he was unsure of what
to do with.

THIRTY-FOUR

When Clint got back to the Black Ace Hotel there was a telegram waiting for him from Howard Haskell. It said that both he and Keith Abel would be on the seven p.m. train the next day, and he wanted Clint to meet them at the station. Clint decided there was nothing left for him to do until then, so he decided to spend some time in the Portsmouth Square casinos, not looking for Beatrice Haskell and Frank Gardner, but just gambling and having a good time. He went upstairs to change into some fresh clothes and left the telegram behind when he left the room.

It was in the Lazy Diamond Casino that Clint ran into Diamond Jack Vincent, who he knew slightly.

"Clint Adams," Vincent said, "I haven't seen you since that game in Denver—what, six years ago?"

"I didn't play in that game, Jack," Clint said, "but it was about six years ago, yeah. Why am I not surprised to find you in the Lazy Diamond?"

Diamond Jack Vincent laughed.

"I have to admit I do sort of like this place," he said.

"Do they still call you Diamond Jack?"

"Yeah, they still do," Vincent said. "Do they still call you the Gunsmith?"

127

"Not to my face, so much. Hey, I heard you played in a game with a fella named Frank Gardner."

"That's right, I did."

"And he won?" Clint asked. "Is he in your class?"

"He was very lucky," Vincent said. "I heard he's been invited into a game that starts tomorrow night at the Alhambra."

"The Alhambra," Clint said. "Last time I was here I had some trouble there with a fella named Frate."

"I heard that Frate wasn't there anymore," Vincent said. "Didn't know you had anything to do with it."

"Are you in that game, too?"

Vincent smiled.

"Wasn't invited, but I'm working on it. He's got a lovely young girl with him."

"Beatrice Haskell."

"You know her," Vincent said in surprise.

"Since she was a little girl," Clint said. "Her father's a friend of mine. She took off with Gardner and didn't tell him where she was going."

"So you found her?"

Clint nodded.

"And told her old man where she is?"

He nodded again.

"I thought there was something wrong there," Vincent said.

"How so?"

"He doesn't pay any attention to her," Vincent said. "She stays in the room all the time—except for today."

"What happened today?"

"I showed her around Portsmouth Square."

"Oh, so that was you. I offered, but she turned me down."

"Sorry. Have you met Gardner?"

"Just today."

"What did you think of him?"

"Didn't like him."

"Why not?"

"He has an attitude. Is he any good at poker?"

"He knows the game," Vincent said, "but without luck he wouldn't have lasted until the end."

Clint wondered if this was just sour grapes on Vincent's part or if he was being honest in his estimation of Gardner's abilities.

"Well, I hope you get into that game and get a chance to recoup some of your losses," Clint said.

"I've already recouped most of them here," Vincent said. "Got lucky at blackjack."

"Well, this is your place, isn't it?" Clint asked.

"I like it here," Vincent said again, "and I'm lucky here."

"And you wouldn't happen to own a little piece of it, would you?"

Vincent smiled and said, "Maybe just a little piece."

"I'm curious," Clint said. "Are you going to continue to show Beatrice around town?"

"Well," Diamond Jack said, "I offered, but I don't know if she's going to take me up on it or not."

"Aren't you afraid Gardner will object?"

"You know," Vincent said, "I don't think he would. I kind of get the feeling he's waiting for somebody to take her off his hands."

"He didn't seem upset when he found out I was here on her father's behalf."

"There you go," Vincent said. "He's waiting for her father to come and get her."

"She doesn't want to go back to El Paso, though."

"Well, who can blame her? How hard a choice is that to make? El Paso? San Francisco?" Vincent made as if he were weighing both choices in separate hands—and suddenly the San Francisco hand plunged down.

"You're right about that. Well, I'd better get some gambling done. When her father gets here I think my job will be done, and I'll want to move on."

"Maybe you'll get lucky and stay awhile," Vincent said. "You know, I remember now that you weren't in that game in Denver. In fact, you and I have never played against each other, have we?"

"No," Clint said, "as a matter of fact we haven't."

"I have an idea."

"And what would that be?"

"How would you like me to get you into that game at the Alhambra?"

Clint was about to decline, but then thought better of it.

"You know," he said, "that might be interesting. Think you can do it?"

"If I can get me in," Vincent said, "then I can get you in."

Clint thought for another moment, then nodded and said, "Why don't you give it a try and see what happens?"

"Excellent!" Vincent said. "Now I'm really looking forward to this."

"You know what?" Clint said. "I kind of am, too, all of a sudden."

THIRTY-FIVE

Clint spent that night with Eileen, as she magically appeared at the Black Ace around midnight. He didn't ask what she did with herself all day. It didn't really matter. He also didn't know if she was married. That didn't seem to matter, either. When she arrived they simply hurried up to his room, got out of their clothes as quickly as possible, and leaped into bed together.

Clint lost himself for hours in her opulent curves, her warm skin, which became more and more moist the longer they strained at each other. She seemed to luxuriate in either sucking him or riding him, either way enjoying being the one on top. Clint put up with that for as long as he could, then flipped her over onto her belly, from where he had an excellent view of her big, firm butt. He slid between her thighs, then, as she rose onto her hands and knees, and drove into her wonderfully wet, hot vagina, wetting himself thoroughly, then withdrawing, spreading the cheeks of her beautiful ass and then sliding between them. He began to move slowly, at first, to make sure he wasn't hurting her, then more and more quickly, and she began to grunt and grown and press back against him, the smooth globes of her butt bouncing off his belly with each thrust. They both began to sweat—well, he was sweating, she was glisten-

131

ing—as their movements became more and more frantic.
"Frantic" seemed to be the word that best described their
"relationship" to this point—the sum total of which so far
had been two nights—or a night and a half—of simply
unbridled lust for each other.

Which suited them both just fine.

"Oh, God," she said later, lying on her back. "I can't seem
to catch my breath."

"Neither can I."

"You know," she said, "if we're around each other any
more we might kill each other."

"I guess we'll just have to limit our contact to the nights
and continue to go our separate ways during the days."

"Live our own lives," she said.

"Right."

She caught a bead of sweat on the tip of her nose with
her index finger.

"Women are supposed to glisten," she said, not com-
plaining at all, "but you make me sweat like a pig."

"That's okay," he said, "you make me grunt like one."

"You know," she said, "I saw you last night and I never
wanted a man as badly as I wanted you—and tonight was
just . . . well, worse. All the way over here I was . . . moist.
It was embarrassing."

"Not too embarrassing, I hope."

"Well, not embarrassing enough to send me back home
to . . ."

"To?"

"Never mind."

"Ah."

So she was married, after all.

THIRTY-SIX

Clint was surprised the next morning when Beatrice entered the dining room of the Black Ace Hotel while he was having breakfast. He waved to her, assuming she'd be there for no other reason than looking for him, and she walked over slowly, calmly, and sat down.

"Coffee?" he asked.

"Yes, please."

"Have you had breakfast?"

"No."

"Would you like to?"

"All right."

Clint waved to the waiter, who came over and took her order.

"What can I do for you, Bea?" he asked. "Besides breakfast, I mean."

"I just wanted you to know that we're not going anywhere."

"That's good."

"We'll be here to see Dad when he comes in."

"That's good, too," he said. "That will make him very happy."

"Are you surprised?"

"No," he said. "I didn't think you'd go anywhere in the first place."

"And Frank?"

"I haven't known him long enough to be surprised by anything he does. I'm just glad it's all working out this way."

"I don't know if it's all working out," she said. "I'm not going back to El Paso."

"At least you'll tell your father that face-to-face," he said, "and he'll know that you're all right. That's all he wants, I think."

"If you think that," she said, "then you don't know my father."

"What do you mean?"

"He'll want me back," she said. "He wants to control me. Wants me to get married in El Paso, live in his house, give him grandchildren, with no thought about what I want. That's the kind of man he is."

"That doesn't sound like the Howard Haskell I know," Clint said.

"You haven't seen him in ten years, Clint," she said. "He's as different now from then as I am."

Well, that was possible. Clint hadn't spent enough time with Haskell in El Paso to make a determination. He was going to have to take Beatrice's word for it.

"Well," Clint said, "it sounds like you and he will have a lot of talking to do."

The waiter came over and served them both their breakfasts.

"I hope that's all we do," she said ominously, "talk."

Later he'd wonder why he hadn't asked her what she meant by that.

After breakfast he walked her out to the lobby.

"When is he coming in?" she asked.

"Tonight," he said. "I'll be meeting him at the station. I'll bring him here first, to check in."

"He won't want to stay here," she said. "It's not nice enough for him."

"It's a perfectly good hotel, Bea."

She shook her head.

"It's not good enough for him. He'll make you take him to the Alhambra or someplace like it. You'll see. Well, I'll be at the St. Charles, whenever he wants to come over and . . . talk. See you later, Clint."

He watched her walk out the front door, resigned to her fate—but what fate was it? Battling her father and staying in San Francisco, with or without Frank Gardner? Or going back to El Paso with her father?

He could only wait and see.

THIRTY-SEVEN

Clint was at the train station at 6:45, just in case the train got in early. It didn't. In fact, it got in fifteen minutes late. He waited on the platform until he saw Haskell get off with Keith Abel, and then he approached them.

"Howard," he said, shaking hands with his friend. "Hello, Keith."

"Clint."

"Where is she?" Haskell asked.

"She's staying at the St. Charles."

"With him?"

"Yes."

"I want to see her."

"I thought we'd get you checked into the hotel first. I'm staying at the Black Ace. They have rooms available."

"Is that in Portsmouth Square?" Haskell asked.

"Just outside it."

"Well," the older man said with a wave of his hand, "you put Keith in there, but take me to the Arcade."

Beatrice had been right about that. The Arcade was on a par with the Alhambra.

"All right, Howard," Clint said. "Let me take your bag—"

"I can carry my own bag," Haskell insisted. "I'm not that old. Do you have a carriage?"

"I do."

"Then let's get going," Haskell said. "I want to see my daughter."

Haskell moved on ahead of the two younger men.

"He's upset," Keith said, making excuses for his boss, "and he's nervous about seeing her."

"Well, she's nervous about seeing him, too."

"How is she?" Keith asked.

"She's fine, physically," he said. "I think she's a little mixed-up, though."

Keith laughed and said, "She always has been. She's always needed the boss to tell her what to do."

"Well, I don't think she wants to be told what to do this time."

"Sure she does," Keith said. "After all, she's letting that gambler tell her what to do, isn't she?"

"I don't think—"

"She just needs to get back on track," Keith said, "and that's what we're here for."

Clint wondered just what "we" meant. How involved was Keith with Beatrice?

They both hurried to catch up with Haskell.

Clint walked Howard Haskell into the Arcade and got him registered.

"I'll take Keith over to the Black Ace and then come back for you," he promised.

"Hurry it up," Haskell said. "I want to see her."

"Don't you want to rest after your long trip?" Clint asked. To him Haskell looked drawn and pale and a good ten years older than when he'd seen him in El Paso.

"I don't need to rest," Haskell said. "I need to see my daughter, set her straight, and take her home. Now you hurry it up."

He allowed a bellboy to carry his bag to the second floor

of the hotel, but he was right behind him, rushing him along.

When they got to the Black Ace, Clint quickly got Keith a room. He was trying to get away from the younger man before he could ask him if he'd remembered his father. The truth of the matter was that it had come to him earlier in the day where and when he'd met Jack Abel, and it was not a pretty story.

"Are you going to go with Howard to see Beatrice?" Clint asked.

"Not tonight," Keith said. "He wants to see her alone. I'll stay here while you take him over there."

"That's fine," Clint said. "Then I'll talk to you later."

He quickly left the Black Ace, leaving Abel to be taken to his room.

Back at the Arcade, Howard Haskell was waiting impatiently in the lobby when Clint arrived.

"It's about time," he said. "Let's go."

"Howard," Clint said, "are you sure you don't want to wait awhile? You seem pretty worked up—"

"Wouldn't you be worked up if some tinhorn gambler took away your only daughter?"

"He didn't kidnap her, Howard," Clint said. "According to what she told me it was her idea to leave without telling you."

"Bah!" Haskell said. "I don't believe that for a minute. He's got control of her mind, Clint. That's obvious. She used to listen to me, do everything I told her—then he came along."

In other words, Clint thought, you used to control her mind, and you're upset because another man has taken it away from you.

Maybe this wasn't the Howard Haskell he knew ten years ago.

THIRTY-EIGHT

When they entered the lobby of the St. Charles, Howard Haskell gave it the once-over and made a face.

"She's staying here?" he asked. "That gambler couldn't do better?"

"This is a nice hotel, Howard," Clint said.

"For some people, maybe," Haskell said.

"Howard," Clint said, "I've got to tell you, you're not acting the way I thought you would."

"And how did you think I would act?" Haskell asked.

"I thought you'd be glad I found Beatrice. I thought you'd be happy to see her."

"Clint," Haskell said, "I'm very grateful that you found her, but she is an ungrateful child. I'm not just going to take her home with me, you know. She's going to have to earn it."

"Earn it?" Clint said. "Howard, she doesn't want to go home."

"We'll see."

Clint stared at Haskell for a few moments.

"What's wrong?" the older man asked.

"I didn't notice it in El Paso, Howard," Clint said, "but you've changed a lot over the past ten years."

"A lot can happen in ten years, Clint," Haskell said.

"I'm sure you're not the same man you were then, either."

"You're probably right about that, Howard," Clint said. "Why don't you wait here, and I'll go up and get her."

"Why don't we just go up to her room?"

"Because I don't want to surprise her," Clint said, "and because I have the feeling this little reunion should take place in public."

"Are you thinking I'll make a scene?"

"I'm thinking you have a gun under your jacket, Howard," Clint said. "In a shoulder rig. That's something new for you."

"What makes you say that?"

"Because you're uncomfortable in it," Clint said. "You keep shrugging your shoulders, like it's chaffing you."

"Never mind that," Haskell said, shrugging his shoulders. "You go up and get her. Let's get this nonsense over with. I have a ranch to run."

"I'll get her and bring her down. Have a seat and wait here."

Haskell looked around, then back at Clint.

"I'll stand," he said.

Clint knocked on the door of Beatrice's room, wondering if Gardner was there with her. When she opened the door she seemed surprised to see Clint—or surprised to see him standing there alone.

"Where is he?" she asked.

"In the lobby," Clint said. "I thought this would be better done in public."

"How is he?"

"Like you said," Clint admitted, "he's different. I didn't notice it in El Paso."

"I told you."

"Yes, you did."

"Well," she said, "let's go."

"You're ready?"

"I've been waiting all day." She stepped out into the hall.

"Where's Gardner?"

"We decided I should talk to my father alone," she said. "He's come here for me, not for Frank."

"I wouldn't be too sure about that."

"What do you mean?"

"He's wearing a gun in a shoulder rig under his jacket."

"Then that's even more of a reason for me to see him alone."

"I agree, Bea," Clint said. "I'm starting to agree with a lot of what you said."

"You mean you're on my side now?"

"I don't want to take sides," Clint said. "I just want whatever happens to be right."

"Well," she said, taking a deep breath, "take me downstairs and let's see what happens."

THIRTY-NINE

As they reached the lobby, Clint held back while Beatrice approached her father. He had expected an embrace of some kind, even a brief one, but instead father and daughter simply stood there, staring at each other. It was as if it was a contest to see who would break and speak first.

Finally, Howard Haskell spoke, perhaps a small victory for his daughter.

"Are you ready to come home?"

"No, Dad."

"Are you still with that . . . gambler?"

"I'm with Frank, yes."

Haskell made a show of looking around the lobby of the St. Charles.

"He can't put you in a better hotel?"

"We like this hotel, Dad."

Clint felt like an eavesdropper, but the truth of the matter was that he was. He didn't want to miss a word.

"Where is he?"

"He's out."

"Is he taking care of you?"

"We're taking care of each other."

"Bah!" Haskell said. "You can't take care of yourself, Beatrice; how can you take care of anyone else?"

145

"You never thought I could do anything, Dad," Beatrice said. "Not since Mother died. I did this to show you that you were wrong."

"All right, then," Haskell said. "I was wrong. You got it out of your system. Now it's time to go home."

"I'm not going back to El Paso, Dad."

"Come back to the ranch."

"Not there, either."

"Come home, Beatrice!" Haskell shouted, drawing the attention of everyone in the lobby. He immediately lowered his voice. "What do you want to come home, Bea?"

"Nothing," she said, "I want nothing, I want you to let me go."

"This would kill your mother, if she were alive," he said.

"Guilt won't work, Dad," she said. "Besides, if Mother were alive she would let me go."

"She was always too easy with you."

"No," Bea said, "you were just too hard."

Haskell looked around the lobby again, but this time he was just trying to compose himself.

"Where is this gambler?" he demanded. "Where is Gardner? I want to talk to him."

"I told you, he's out," she said. "He'll be back later."

"He's with another woman, isn't he?"

Clint saw Beatrice flinch, as if her father had slapped her.

"You know, Dad, I really don't know for sure. Maybe he is."

"I'll set him straight," Haskell said. "I want to talk to him."

"Do you want to offer him money to leave me?"

"Don't think he wouldn't."

"I don't care," she said. "I don't care if you pay him and he leaves me. I still won't come back home."

"What are you saying?"

"I'm . . . not . . . coming . . . back," she said slowly. "How can I make you understand?"

"I understand that you've lost your *mind*!"

Again, the rising tone of his voice was attracting attention.

"Let's go to my hotel and discuss this," he said then.

"No."

"Fine, then we'll go to your room—"

"No, Father," Beatrice said. "I'm through discussing this. It's over. It's time for you to go home and let me live my life."

"You don't know what you're saying."

"I do."

"You've lost your mind."

"No."

"He's poisoned your mind against me."

"No."

"*Some*thing is wrong here!" he hissed.

She reached out with her hand, as if to touch her father's face. At the same time he pulled back a bit, and she did, and there was no contact. She dropped her arm to her side.

"Good-bye, Father." She turned and walked away from him. She walked past Clint, back up the stairs to her room.

"Go get her," Haskell said to Clint. "Bring her back here. I'm not finished."

"She is, Howard."

"Bring her back, I said."

"I don't take orders, Howard," Clint said. "I found her as a favor to you, but if I'd known how you were going to treat her, I don't think I would have agreed to do so."

"What? What?"

"Take her at her word, Howard," Clint said. "She's a grown woman."

"She's nothing but a child," Haskell said. "She hasn't got the sense she was born with."

"She's no child," Clint said, "and she's got more sense than you give her credit for."

"Are you against me, too?" Haskell demanded.

"Nobody's against you, Howard," Clint said. "I'm not

taking sides, I'm just through. My part is done.''

"I still want to talk to this gambler.''

"I'm sure Bea will tell him that, and I'm sure he'll come and see you. Why don't you let me take you back to your hotel?''

"I don't need to be taken back," Haskell said. "I can make my own way.''

"Suit yourself.''

Haskell pointed a finger at Clint and said, "We are no longer friends.''

Clint smiled without any humor and said, "I think I already knew that, Howard.''

Haskell glowered at him, then turned and marched out of the hotel. Clint could hear him shouting at the cab driver out front. Clint had hired the cab, but he let Haskell take it. He could walk back to the Black Ace. The air would clear his head. Once it was clear he hoped that he would stick to his guns and not take sides.

Like he had told Howard Haskell, his part in all this was finished.

He was done.

FORTY

"So you're finished?" Dilman asked.

"That's what I told him," Clint said.

They were sitting at Dilman's table in the Black Ace dining room sharing a late meal. It was already a foregone conclusion that when Clint ate at Dilman's table he was eating on the house.

"So what will you do now?"

"Stay in San Francisco for a few more days," Clint said. "Enjoy the gambling and the company."

"I'm flattered."

"You're not the company I was talking about."

Dilman laughed and said, "I know. You were referring to Eileen."

"Whose last name I still don't know."

"Is that important?"

Clint stared across the table at Dilman and said, "You tell me."

"Why me?"

"Because you obviously know her," Clint said. "Is her husband someone who's going to come after me if he finds out about us?"

"What makes you think she has a husband?"

"Just a slip," Clint said. "A small thing that I picked up on."

Dilman hesitated, then said, "Well, probably not."

"Will he send someone after me?"

Dilman hesitated again.

"So he has money."

"Let's just say he's ... prominent."

"And does he ever come to Portsmouth Square ... or its fringes?"

"No," Dilman said. "He doesn't gamble ... with money, that is."

"Aha," Clint said. "A politician."

Dilman didn't answer.

"Shouldn't a politician's wife be more discreet?" Clint asked.

"She probably will be," Dilman said, "once he becomes more ... visible."

"So he intends to run for some high office in the future."

Dilman smiled. "You're actually quite good at this, aren't you?" he asked.

"Actually," Clint said, "I hate guessing games."

"Well, as they go," Dilman said, "this one has been a good one."

"Let's play another one," Clint said, looking at the doorway.

"Okay," Dilman said, frowning.

"My guess is that this is a policeman, and he's looking for one of us," Clint said.

Dilman looked and said, "You *are* good at this. That's Inspector Farley."

"And he's coming this way."

"You or me?" Dilman asked.

"I've got twenty dollars that says it's you," Clint said.

"You're on."

"Actually," Clint said, "I'm hoping ...."

"Mr. Dilman," the policeman said, removing his bowler.

He had a handlebar mustache, a tweed three-piece suit, and a gun under his arm.

"Inspector," Dilman said. "To what do I owe this pleasure?"

"Well, sir," Farley said, "I was told I could find a Clint Adams here with you."

"I'm Adams," Clint said.

"You owe me twenty," Dilman said.

"Sir?" Farley asked.

Dilman smiled. "Just a private wager, Inspector."

"Is there something I can do for you, Inspector?" Clint asked.

"Yes, sir," Farley said, "if you'd be so kind as to accompany me to the St. Charles Hotel."

"Why?"

"We have a situation there you might be able to help us with."

"And that situation is?"

"There's been a murder."

"Who's dead?" Clint asked, making a private wager with himself.

"A man named Howard Haskell."

He lost his second bet of the night.

FORTY-ONE

When Clint first saw the inspector he had had the feeling someone was dead, only he thought it was going to be Frank Gardner. He had seen in Howard Haskell such a potential for violence that he had almost been expecting this.

"You don't look surprised, sir," the inspector said.

"Frankly, Inspector," Clint said, "I'm not."

"Why is that?"

"You'd have to understand the entire situation."

"Suppose you explain it to me," the inspector suggested, sitting down.

"Don't we have to get over to the St. Charles?" Clint asked.

"There's no hurry," Farley said. "I have men there, and the deceased isn't going anywhere."

"Before I start," Clint said, "how did you know to come here looking for me?"

"If you mean the dining room, the desk clerk told me you'd be here," Farley said. "If you mean this hotel, the deceased daughter, Beatrice Haskell, asked me to come over here and get you."

"Is she all right?"

"She was hysterical at first," Farley said. "You see, she found her father's body."

153

"Wait," Clint said. "She found his body in his room at the Arcade?"

"No," the policeman said, "in her room at the St. Charles. The room she shares with a man named Frank Gardner."

"And where's Gardner?"

"We don't know."

"Is he a suspect?"

"At this time, sir," Farley said, "everyone is a suspect. Would you like to tell me this story now?"

Clint made it as brief as possible, explaining why he was there, and why Howard Haskell was there. It didn't take long, and the policeman listened in total silence and concentration until he was finished.

"That's all very interesting," he finally said.

"And it seems to point to Gardner even more, doesn't it?" Dilman asked.

"It could."

"I mean, in light of his absence."

"He's a gambler," Clint said. "Maybe he found a game tonight."

"That's possible, too," Farley said, standing up. "Would you come to the St. Charles with me now, Mr. Adams? I believe you could do Miss Haskell some good."

"Of course," Clint said, also standing.

"See you later," Dilman said.

Clint nodded, and he and Inspector Farley left the dining room and the hotel together.

Outside Farley had a carriage waiting and they both got in.

"How was he killed?"

"He was shot, at close range."

"Nobody heard anything?"

"We're asking questions now."

"How did he get into the room?"

"We're trying to find that out, too. We don't know much of anything yet, Mr. Adams."

"When did she find him?"

"About two hours ago."

"She must be frantic by now," Clint said. Her father dead, her lover missing . . .

"Actually," Farley said, "after her initial hysteria she's been quite calm. She has been asking for you, though. How well do you know her?"

"I saw her this week for the first time in ten years," Clint said. "Her father and I are old friends."

"What do you know about Frank Gardner?"

Clint hesitated a moment. Did anything that Dominick Polo had told him about Gardner have any bearing in this incident? After all, Haskell had been shot, not beaten to death, as Jack Abel had been all those years ago.

"I don't know much about him," Clint said. "I only met him for the first time this trip, as well."

"Did you like him?"

"No."

"Why not?"

"It was sort of an immediate thing between us," Clint said. "I didn't like him, and he didn't like me. It was obvious."

"Was he afraid of you?"

"Why would he be?"

"I'm aware of your reputation," Farley said.

"I don't know if he was afraid of me or not."

"Can you usually tell?"

"When it's obvious."

"I would think you'd get a lot of that," Farley said. "Fear, respect . . . I would think they'd be hard to tell apart sometimes."

"They are."

"I'd also think—"

"I don't think a discussion of my reputation has any

bearing on your business tonight, Inspector, do you?''

Farley hesitated, then said, ''You're probably right, Mr. Adams.''

They rode the rest of the way to the St. Charles in silence.

FORTY-TWO

When they reached the St. Charles, Farley led Clint in past some of his men, who were posted outside and questioning people in the lobby.

"Where is she?" Clint asked. "Not in the room—"

"Of course not," Farley said. "The body hasn't been removed yet. She's in the manager's office."

He led Clint past the front desk and down a hallway to an office where Beatrice was sitting in a chair, staring off into space. Someone had covered her with a blanket, but it had fallen down around her waist, and she wasn't bothering to fix it. There was a lone uniformed policeman in the room with her.

"Has she been seen by a doctor?" Clint asked in a low tone.

"The hotel doctor, yes," Farley said. "He said she might be in shock, but she's lucid."

She didn't look very lucid at that moment.

"If I can be alone with her . . ." Clint said.

"Of course. I'll have my man wait outside."

Farley stepped out of the room with his officer.

Clint crouched down in front of Beatrice.

"Bea?"

Suddenly, she focused her eyes on him.

157

"Clint?"

She put her arms around him and he held her tightly to him.

"He's dead," she said fiercely in his ear. "He's dead."

"I know," he said. "I'm sorry."

He held her that way for a while, then drew back, keeping their hands on each other's shoulders. The contact seemed to help her.

"Do you know what happened, Bea?"

"Frank didn't do it," she said. "They think he did, but he didn't."

"Are you sure?"

Tears began streaming down her face and she said, "No," in a shaky voice.

"Do you know where he is, Bea?"

"No," she said. "I told them the truth. He went out and I don't know where he went."

"What were you doing?"

"I was . . ."

"What? You were what?"

She bit her lip and said, "I was with Diamond Jack Vincent."

"Where? In his room?"

"No," she said, shaking her head. "We were in the casino. Frank . . . hadn't taken me to the casino the whole time we were here. Jack took me tonight. I was having a wonderful time while . . . while someone was killing my father."

"Was Jack Vincent with you when you found your father in your room?"

"No," she said. "I was alone."

"All right," Clint said. "Have you answered all their questions truthfully?"

"Y-yes."

"They probably have more to ask you," he said. "Do you feel up to it?"

She grabbed his hand and held it tightly for a few moments before answering.

"Will you stay with me?"

"Of course," he said. "The whole time."

"All right, then."

He patted her on the knee and then went out into the hall.

"Inspector?" he called. "She can answer more questions for you now."

FORTY-THREE

Clint stood alongside Beatrice while she answered all of the inspector's questions. She hadn't seen or spoken to her father since she left him in the lobby. She didn't know where Frank Gardner was, but she didn't think he would kill her father.

"Even if he did," she added, "he wouldn't do it in our room, would he? And then leave the body there?"

"He would if he was going to run afterwards," Farley said.

"We don't know that he's on the run, Inspector," Clint said.

"With all due respect, Mr. Adams," Farley said, "we don't know that he isn't." He looked at Beatrice. "Miss Haskell, we've removed the body from the room, but I don't think you'll be wanting to go back into that room tonight, will you?"

"No!" she said emphatically.

"I don't even think she should stay in this hotel tonight, Inspector," Clint said. "I'll take her back to the Black Ace with me and get her a room."

"How will Frank find me?" she asked.

Clint put his hand on her shoulder and said, "He'll figure it out."

"Besides," Farley said, "I'll have men waiting for him in the lobby. If and when he gets back they'll gra—uh, let him know what's happened."

Clint was impressed. This was the first indication he'd had that the inspector knew what tact was.

"Can she go, Inspector?"

"Sure," he said. "I'll know where she is . . . won't I?"

"She'll be at the Black Ace," Clint said. "Come on, Bea."

He helped her up, leaving the blanket behind, and they left the St. Charles together.

Clint unlocked the door to her new room at the Black Ace and let her go in ahead of him.

"You must be exhausted," he said.

"I don't know," she said. "I'm too numb to feel exhausted."

"You'd better get to bed and get some rest," he said, pulling the bedclothes down.

"Clint . . ." Whatever she was going to say she seemed to tired to continue.

"Come on," he said, "get out of those clothes and into bed."

"Are you going to leave?"

"Well, you have to get undressed. . . ."

"I'll just drop my clothes here and get into bed," she said. "I'm not shy. You're like . . . an uncle."

Without hesitation she removed all of her clothes, revealing herself to be much fuller and firmer when naked than she looked when she was dressed. Clint looked away, feeling like a dirty old man now that she had told him he was like her uncle.

"All right," she said, and when he looked back she was in bed.

"I'm in room seven, just down the hall," he said, "if you need anything during the night."

"All right," she said, her eyelids growing heavier. "Thank you, Clint, for being here."

"It's going to be all right, Bea," he said, kissing her forehead. "You'll be fine."

"I'll be fine," she repeated, "but my father is dead, and my lover is missing. . . ."

"It'll all sort itself out," he said, "I promise."

He turned the gas lamp on the wall down. She was asleep before he left the room.

FORTY-FOUR

Clint found Dilman in the casino and filled him in on everything that had happened.

"She's in the room now," he finished. "I told her I'd be in mine, so that's where I'm going."

"Thanks for filling me in," Dilman said. "Don't worry about the cost of her room. It'll be my donation."

"Thanks, Case."

"Sure. Let me know if there's anything else I can do, Clint."

"I will."

Clint left the casino and went to his room. At the door he stopped and saw a light under the door. Whoever was inside was not making any secret of it. It could have been Eileen, but just in case he drew his gun, fit the key into the lock, and opened the door quickly.

"You won't need that," Frank Gardner said, raising his hands.

"Where's your gun?" Clint asked.

"I thought you'd ask me that," Gardner said. He inclined his head and Clint looked in that direction. A short-barreled revolver was sitting on the top of the dresser.

"Derringer?"

"Don't carry one," Gardner said. "Honest, I'm unarmed now."

"Put your arms up higher," Clint said, closing the door but keeping his gun on the gambler.

He approached Gardner, patted him down, and found that he was telling the truth. He was, indeed, unarmed.

Clint backed up and holstered his gun.

"What are you doing in my room?"

"I didn't have anyplace else to go," Gardner said. "I didn't kill Haskell."

"How do you know he's dead?"

"I came back to the hotel and saw all the police. I got close enough to hear two of them talking. Can I put my hands down?"

"Put them down and sit on the bed," Clint said. He grabbed a straight-backed wooden chair, turned it around, and straddled it.

"What do you want here?"

"Help."

"Why should I help you?"

"For Bea's sake."

"You haven't even asked me how she is, or where she is. How worried can you be about her?"

"She's not suspected of murder," he pointed out. "I am."

"So talk to the police."

"They'll arrest me on sight."

"What makes you think that?"

"I had a motive."

"Did you see Haskell since he got to San Francisco?" Clint asked.

"No."

"Is that the truth?"

"Yes."

If Gardner was lying then he was probably a good poker player, too.

"So if it wasn't Bea and it wasn't you, who was it?" Clint asked. "And why in your room?"

"To frame me."

"Who'd want to do that?"

"I don't know."

Clint thought a moment, then said, "There's a joker in this deck."

"Who's that?"

"Keith Abel."

"The foreman? Is he here?"

"He is. He came in with Haskell."

"Well, there you go," Gardner said. "He's in love with Bea. He'd have reason to frame me."

"So why would he kill her father?"

"Because that would get rid of both of us. He could have Bea and the ranch."

"That's a possibility," Clint said.

"Where is he?"

"I don't know," Clint said. "He's got a room in this hotel."

"It had to be him," Gardner said. "Who else could it be?"

"And maybe he has more of a motive than you think," Clint said.

"What's that mean?"

"He's Jack Abel's son."

"Who's Jack Abel?"

"The man you and some other gamblers beat to death twenty years ago in Caldwell, Kansas, for cheating—before you changed your name, Mr. Gleason."

Gardner froze.

"How did you know that?"

"It doesn't matter," Clint said. "If I know, then maybe Haskell and Keith knew as well."

"I was there," Gardner said, "but I never touched the man."

"Why did you change your name, then?"

"I told you," Gardner said, "I was there. I didn't kill him, but I didn't try to stop it, either."

"I don't think Keith would care about that," Clint said. "But this man doesn't strike me as a killer."

"Haskell sent you after us, right?"

"Right."

"Did you see the real Haskell?"

Clint hesitated, then said, "No, not until he got here."

"Then maybe you haven't seen the real Keith Abel, either," Gardner said. He shook his head. "Abel. I never put those two together."

"I don't see how Keith could know about you," Clint said, "unless . . ."

"Unless what?"

"Unless Haskell hired a private detective to check into your background. That's how I got on to you."

"And I thought changing my name would keep that from ever happening."

"But if Haskell knew your background, why not tell me?" Clint wondered aloud.

"Maybe he didn't think it had to do with Bea and me," Gardner offered. "Adams, I need a place to stay."

"Not here," Clint said.

"What about Bea? Where is she?"

Clint decided not to tell Gardner that she was in this hotel.

"She's at the St. Charles."

"Not in that room."

"No, they gave her another one."

"I can't get into that hotel with the police there," Gardner said. "What should I do?"

"Get a room as far from the Square as you can. Send me word where you are, and then wait to hear from me."

"You'll help me?"

"I'll help Bea," Clint said. "If that helps you at the same time . . ." He shrugged.

Gardner stood up.

"But where should I go?"

"Go down to the Barbary Coast. Take a room in a hotel there."

"For how long?"

"Until I figure this out," Clint said, "or until the police catch the killer."

Gardner frowned.

"You won't tell the police where I am?"

"Not unless I decide you did it."

Gardner's frown deepened.

"You asked me for help, Gardner," Clint said. "You're just going to have to trust me."

"I guess I have no choice."

"None," Clint said.

FORTY-FIVE

Once Gardner was gone Clint felt no guilt about turning
him out. He didn't owe the man anything. Howard Haskell
was his friend, and Beatrice was the one he had to look out
for. For all he knew Gardner was lying to him and had
killed Haskell. If he had he'd pay the price, but if he hadn't
then there was someone else out there who owed for it.

Could it have been Keith Abel?

That was a question he would put to Beatrice in the
morning. The other thing he had to do come morning was
find Abel himself and talk to him. If the man wasn't the
killer, then he still didn't know that his boss was dead. It
would come as a shock.

Clint decided to turn in himself, because there was nothing to be done until morning.

In the morning he woke and went right to Beatrice's room.
When he knocked she called out, "Come in."

She was still in bed, with the sheet molded to her naked
body.

"I need some clothes," she said. "Could you go back
to the hotel and get me some?"

"Sure," he said, "then we can have some breakfast.
What would you like me to bring?"

She gave him a sheepish look and said, "Everything?"

• • •

Clint had to check with the policemen on duty in the lobby, and luckily one of them was the one who had been in the office with her. He seemed to have become smitten with her and told Clint he could get her clothes, but that he'd have to go into the room with him. Clint said that was fine.

When he returned to the Black Ace with Bea's clothes, he deposited them on the bed. She was still lying under the sheet. He could see how full her breasts were and that her nipples were hard, presumably because she was cold.

"I'll meet you down in the dining room, Bea," he said, and got out of there before he stopped thinking like an uncle.

When Bea came down to the dining room, Clint had a pot of coffee on the table and two cups. As she approached he poured her some.

"Thank you," she said.

"I waited for you to order."

"That was sweet."

"How are you feeling this morning?"

"Well," she said, putting the cup down, "when I woke up I felt wonderful. It was amazing, I felt so refreshed—and then it all came rushing back and I felt awful for feeling so good."

Clint didn't know what to say to that, so he decided to get to the point—but first they ordered breakfast.

"Gardner came to see me last night," he said when the waiter had gone.

"Frank? Here? Did you tell him—"

"I didn't have to tell him about your father," he said. "He knew."

"How?"

"He said he saw all the police at the hotel and heard them talking."

"Why didn't he come in?"

"He knew he'd be suspected."

"Why didn't he come and see me last night?"

"I didn't tell him you were here."

"Why not?"

"It was a spur-of-the-moment decision," Clint said. "I'm . . . not sure about him, Bea. I just didn't want the two of you getting together for a while."

"Did you ask him if he killed my father?"

"I did, and he said no."

"I knew he didn't."

"You have to understand why the police would suspect him, Bea," Clint said. "He and your father did not get along."

"It had to be somebody else," she said firmly. "It had to be."

"Like who?"

She groped for some words and finally blurted, "I don't know."

"Bea," he said, "how about Keith Abel?"

"Keith? Why would he kill my father?"

"I don't know why he'd kill your father, but he has a motive for framing Frank for it."

"What motive could he possibly have?"

Clint hesitated, then said, "Keith's father was a man named Jack Abel. Twenty years ago he was caught cheating in a poker game. The players dragged him outside and beat him to death."

"Oh, my God," she said, "but what does that have to do with Frank?"

"Back then Frank's name was Gleason, and he was one of the players."

"Oh, my *God*!" she said again. "He couldn't have—what does he say?"

"He says he was there, but that he didn't participate. He also says he didn't try to stop it, so he changed his name."

"How would Keith know this?"

"I found out through a private detective," Clint said. "If

your father had Frank investigated he would have found out, too, and told Keith.''

"And is Keith here?''

"He came in with your father.''

She sat forward in her chair.

"So my father brought Keith here so he could kill Frank,'' she said.

"And maybe,'' Clint said, taking up the string, "instead of killing Gardner he killed your father and tried to frame Gardner for it.''

"What would be his motive for all that?'' she asked. "Why not just kill Frank for what he did?''

"Maybe,'' Clint said, looking at her carefully, "he did it to get the girl, too.''

From the look on her face he knew he'd hit a nerve.

"Do you want to tell me about it, Bea?''

FORTY-SIX

"There's nothing to tell."

"Does Keith want you?"

She hesitated, then said, "Yes."

"And how did your father feel about that?"

"He told Keith a long time ago he wasn't good enough for me," she said.

"How long ago?"

"Years."

"And Keith accepted that?" Clint thought he knew how Doc Holliday must have felt back in the days when he was a dentist and pulling teeth.

"Yes."

"How did you feel about it? Did you want Keith, at all?"

"Once," she said, "I thought I did, but he was . . . my first. I soon learned that I didn't really want him, after all."

"When was that?" he asked. "Before or after you met Gardner?"

"After," she said. "That was when I learned what it was like to be with a . . . a man."

"So after your father told Keith he wasn't good enough for you," Clint asked, "he just went on working for your father?"

"Yes."

"He accepted it rather easily, didn't he?"

"I thought he did," she said, "but now I realize maybe he didn't."

"You think he was planning something like this all along?"

"I—I don't know what to think."

"I think maybe the plan formed in his mind once you met Gardner," Clint said. "He saw a way to get rid of both of the men in your life that were keeping you from him—and at the same time he could take revenge on one of the men who killed his father."

She remained silent for a few minutes, then shook her head and said, "Poor Keith."

"Why poor Keith? He might be the man who killed your father, Bea."

"But what about what happened to his father? He had to live with that all these years. Was his father a card cheat, Clint?"

"I told Keith I had met his father sometime, but I couldn't remember where or when."

"And now you do?"

"I still don't remember where it was," Clint said, "but it was a few years before he was killed."

"What happened?"

"I caught him cheating at cards."

"Oh, God. Are you going to tell Keith this?"

"I wasn't sure whether I was or not, but that may not matter anymore, Bea," Clint sad. "If he killed your father he's got much bigger problems."

"Where is Frank?" she asked.

"He's in a hotel down on the Barbary Coast. I told him to stay out of sight until I can figure out what's going on."

"And how are you going to do that?"

"I'm going to have to find Keith."

"And how are you going to do that?"

"Well," Clint said, "if he killed your father and thinks

he's successfully framed Frank Gardner for it, he should be up in his room.''

"In this hotel?"

"Yes."

She pushed her chair back.

"Then let's go and see."

He reached across the table and grabbed her arm to stop her.

"I think you should wait here, Bea. I'll go and see."

"Why can't I come?"

"Because he may not want to come peacefully."

"You mean you might have to . . . shoot him?"

"I hope not," Clint said. "I hope he doesn't try to use his gun."

"I can keep him from doing it," she said.

"I don't think so," Clint said. "Just as you proved to me that I didn't know the man your father had become, I don't think you know the man Keith has become. I want you to stay here."

"Clint—"

"Can I help?"

They both looked up and saw Case Dilman standing by their table.

"Is this man causing you some trouble, ma'am?" Dilman asked, joking.

"No, I—it's just—"

"Bea," Clint said, "this is Case Dilman. He owns the Black Ace."

"Oh," she said, as Clint released her arm, "hello."

"Miss Haskell," Dilman said, "I was very sorry to hear about your father."

"Thank you."

"If there's anything I can do—"

"There's one thing you can do for me," Clint said, standing up.

"What's that?"

"Keep her here!"

"Clint!" she shouted. "Don't you dare!"

"Clint?"

"Case," he said, "keep her here. It's important. Don't let her leave."

"Clint Adams, you come back here!"

She started to get up, but Case put one hand on her shoulder.

"Don't you touch me."

"Then don't make me, Miss Haskell. Let's just sit here quietly and wait for Clint to come back."

"You don't understand," she said. "Someone might get killed."

"Why don't you tell me about it," Dilman said.

FORTY-SEVEN

When Clint knocked on the door of Keith Abel's room, the man called out, "Who's there?"

It didn't prove anything, but Clint felt justified in leaving Bea downstairs.

"It's Clint Adams, Keith."

There was a moment of hesitation and then Abel said, "Come on in."

Clint opened the door and stepped in. Abel was sitting in a chair by the window.

"Good morning," Abel said.

"Morning."

Clint closed the door.

"What can I do for you?" Abel asked. "I was about to go over to the Arcade and see what was happening with the boss. You want to come?"

"I've been over there."

"You have? Did you see the boss?"

"He's dead."

"What?" Abel froze in his chair. "What did you say?"

"I said he's dead, Keith," Clint said. "Somebody killed him."

"That can't be," the younger man said. "Jesus. Have you told Beatrice?"

"She's the one who found him."

"Oh, my God," he said, coming out of his chair. "She must be a wreck. Where is she?"

"She's all right," Clint said. "She spent the night here in the hotel."

"Spent the night? When did this happen?"

"Last night."

"Why didn't anyone tell me?"

"Well," Clint said, "I was more concerned with Bea, and the police are concerned with finding Frank Gardner."

"That son of a bitch," Abel said. "He did it, didn't he?"

"I don't know. They think so."

"Son of a bitch," Abel said again. "I'll kill him."

"I thought you'd like to know, Keith, that I remember where I knew your dad."

"What? My father? Where?"

"We played poker once, years ago."

"You did? Was he as good as I always heard he was?"

"He was a cheat, Keith."

"What?"

"Yeah," Clint said, "I caught him cheating."

"No," Abel said, "that can't be."

"It was," Clint said. "It was a couple of years before . . . before that last time. He finally got caught for the last time."

"You mean . . ."

"I mean maybe he didn't deserve to be beaten to death," Clint said, "but he was cheating that day."

Abel fell quiet and just stared.

"Gardner was there," Clint said.

"He was?"

"Only he was called Gleason then."

"Gleason."

"But you knew that already, didn't you?"

"I—what?" Abel seemed puzzled.

"Howard must have had Gardner investigated," Clint said. "If he did, then he found out about his name change and the reason for it—and he probably told you.''

''What are you . . . talking about?''

''I think you know.''

Abel turned and looked out the window.

''Bea told me you were her first boyfriend, Keith,'' he went on.

''Did she also tell you her father wouldn't let us be together?''

''Yes.''

''Said I wasn't good enough.''

''I heard.''

Abel turned from the window.

''Do you know what else he told me?''

''What?''

''After his detective told him about Gardner? And my father? He said he was right not to let me be with his daughter. After all, I was the son of a card cheat.''

''Did you want to kill him?''

''Right there and then.''

''But you didn't.''

''No.''

''You waited for the right time.''

''Huh?''

''The right place.''

''What?''

''And the right man to pin it on—Gardner.''

''Gleason.''

''Right,'' Clint said, ''Gleason.''

''Are you sayin'—''

''That you killed Howard Haskell,'' Clint said. ''That's what I'm saying.''

''That's crazy,'' Keith Abel said. ''The police know Gardner did it. They found the body in his hotel room.''

''How did you know that?''

''What?''

''How did you know they found the body in Gardner's room?''

"You—you just told me."

"No, I didn't," Clint said. "I told you Haskell was dead, but I deliberately didn't say where he was found. You know because that's where you killed him. You both probably went up there to confront Gardner. When he didn't answer the door you forced it. Once inside, you killed Haskell and left the body there to frame Gardner—only Bea found him first."

Clint stopped talking then, and there were a few long moments of silence before Abel finally spoke.

"Poor Bea."

Clint thought that was ironic. Just a little while ago Bea was saying, "Poor Keith."

"I did it for her, you know."

"For her?"

He nodded. "It was the only way she'd be rid of him, the only way we could be together on the ranch."

"But she doesn't want to be together," Clint said. "She doesn't want you, and she doesn't want the ranch."

"She wants Gardner," Abel said tightly.

"Maybe," Clint said, "but mostly she doesn't want to go back to El Paso or the ranch."

"She will," Abel said, "she will, when this is all over. When the police have Gardner."

"The police aren't going to arrest Gardner, Keith."

"Why not?"

"Because I'm going to tell them it was you."

Abel wasn't wearing a gun. Clint had noticed that as soon as he walked in. When he turned away from the window, however, he was holding one. Clint realized that when he knocked on the door Abel must have put his gun on the windowsill.

Now he cocked the hammer.

"You're not going to tell anyone anything."

"Don't be foolish, Keith," Clint said, his stomach muscles clenching, preparing for the bullet. He felt foolish at having been taken this way. He felt old. "People know I'm here. Bea knows I'm here."

"I'll tell them—I'll tell them—"

"Tell them what?" Clint asked. "That I killed Haskell?"

"You and Gardner . . ."

"You're going to try to frame us for the same murder? Can't be done, Keith. It's all over now. Even if you kill me, Bea knows you did it. She's probably telling the police right now."

"She . . . wouldn't . . ."

"Yes, she would," Clint said. "She doesn't want to be with you, Keith. When will you get that through your thick head?"

"No . . ."

"Go ahead," Clint said, "pull the trigger. It won't be a surprise like it was with Haskell. You'll have to shoot me while I'm looking right at you, Keith. Come on. Pull it. The shot's bound to bring somebody. This is not a big hotel like the St. Charles, where a single shot might go unnoticed. You pull that trigger and the room will be filled with people, and you can't kill them all."

"My father . . ." Abel said, tears streaming down his face. "Was he really a cheat?"

"Yes, Keith, he was."

"Then the boss was right," he said. "I didn't deserve Bea."

"No, he was wrong," Clint said. "If Bea had wanted you, that shouldn't have kept you apart. You're not responsible for what your father did."

Abel wiped the tears away angrily with his other hand, his right hand tightening on the gun.

"But you're responsible for this, Keith," Clint said. "For killing Howard Haskell and for killing me. This is all yours, and this is much worse than cheating at cards."

"Damn it," Keith Abel said, "damn my father, damn the boss, damn Gardner, and damn you . . ."

"And damn you, too, Keith, if you pull that trigger."

"Then damn me . . ." he said.

At that moment someone pounded on the door and Bea shouted, "Keith! Don't!"

"Bea!" Abel said, his eyes flicking toward the door.

Clint couldn't take the chance. Abel was obviously a sick man, inches from taking his life. He did the only thing he could. As soon as Abel's eyes flicked toward the door Clint drew and fired. His bullet caught Keith Abel right in the midsection, drove him back into the window, and then through the glass and out of the room and the hotel.

Clint opened the door and found Bea in the hall with Case Dilman. Bea threw her arms around him and cried.

"I owe you a window," he said to Dilman.

FORTY-EIGHT

Clint didn't waste any time. Once the police were convinced that the killer was dead, he sent word to Frank Gardner. The gambler came back to the St. Charles just long enough to collect his belongings. He said good-bye to Beatrice Haskell, who had nothing to say to him in return. He was the third man who'd once claimed he loved her to leave her in twenty-four hours.

The next morning Clint was ready to leave, too.

"We sat up and talked most of the night," Case Dilman told Clint the next morning at breakfast. "While you were clearing things up with the police."

"And how is she?"

"She's going to stay here for a while," Dilman said. "I offered her a job and she said yes."

"What about the ranch?"

"I have a lawyer here who can help her sell it."

"Sounds like you're going to be a good friend to her, Case."

"She's a lovely young woman," Dilman said, "and she's been through a lot. She needs help."

"I'm glad you've decided to help her."

"What about you?" Dilman asked. "That game starts

tonight, you know. Without you they'll be short two players, you and Gardner.''

"If Bea is okay," Clint said, "I think I'd just rather
move on.''

"Can't say I blame you," Dilman said. "You lost something, too. A friend.''

"I guess the Howard Haskell I was friends with was lost
a long time ago," Clint said. "I'm just sorry I had to kill
Keith. I think he just needed some help, too.''

"What about Gardner? What's he going to do?''

"Well, if history is any judge, I guess he'll go someplace, change his name, and start over again.''

"How many times can you expect that to work?" Dilman asked.

"Not many, I guess.''

"You're not going to leave without saying good-bye to
Beatrice, are you?''

"No," Clint said, "I can wait that long. Is she coming
down to breakfast?''

"She said she would, so we can talk about her job.''

"I'll wait, then.''

"More coffee?''

"Sure.''

"And maybe," Dilman said, pouring, "I can talk you
into staying for that game.''

Clint smiled and said, "No harm in trying, I suppose.''